L

Sarah ... ut the thousand sparks of desire he was igniting. She didn't want to feel these things, but maybe it was time to reclaim a part of her life again.

Shifting, she ended up solidly on top of him, pushing him into the sand. She pressed along the entire length of him, leaving her intentions in no doubt.

Sarah felt a rumble in his chest, a laugh maybe or a groan, as his hands closed over her buttocks. "Smooth move. Someone took some self-defence classes?"

She just smiled, locking her knees around his hips before launching an assault on his mouth.

And then before she could take her next breath, she found herself flipped over on her back. Logan settled between her sprawled legs, his hands pinning hers on either side of her head.

"Pretty smooth yourself," she murmured. "You must have taken those same classes."

"Yeah, something like that."

Sarah stared up at him, wondering what he was planning. Hadn't she made it clear she was willing? *And ready*, she thought, feeling his hardness pressing between her legs. Oh, was she ever ready. She was hot all over, and it wasn't from the midday sun.

This book is dedicated to all those who work every single day to return the Chesapeake Bay Watershed to being a healthy, vibrant environment. You rock.

Many thanks to Michael Perecca for his wonderful "walk through" of the streets of Brooklyn, and for inspiring me to go there to experience it for myself.

Dear Reader,

I hope you are as excited about *Friction* as I am. It was so much fun to get Sarah and Logan together in this book, even if they didn't always make it easy. One of my favourite things about writing for Mills & Boon® Blaze® is that I get to create characters who deal with their deepest fears to discover love. Sarah and Logan certainly face these issues head-on, and with life-changing results.

I wrote this book in the middle of a frosty winter, and it was a treat to visit the summer beaches and waters of the Chesapeake in my imagination while the snow was piling up outside. I hope Sarah and Logan's passionate adventures will warm things up for you, as well!

Please stop by my website, www.samanthahunter.com, and see what's new.

Samantha Hunter

FRICTION

BY
SAMANTHA HUNTER

MILLS & BOON®
Pure reading pleasure

*First published in Great Britain 2007
by Harlequin Mills & Boon Limited,
Eton House, 18-24 Paradise Road, Richmond, Surrey TW9 1SR*

© Samantha Hunter 2006

ISBN: 978 0 263 85594 4

14-1007

*Harlequin Mills & Boon policy is to use papers that are
natural, renewable and recyclable products and made from
wood grown in sustainable forests. The logging and
manufacturing processes conform to the legal environmental
regulations of the country of origin.*

*Printed and bound in Spain
by Litografia Rosés S.A., Barcelona*

1

SARAH JESSUP stretched languorously under the warm rays of the sun. It was late June and the Virginia Beach hotels were already packed. The beach was swarming with vacationers: children scooping sand into red buckets under the watchful eyes of their moms sitting in low chairs planted in the gentle surf and, of course, the see-and-be-seen bikini crowd. And Sarah definitely wanted to be seen.

She'd cut her long, curly, brown hair boy-short for the summer, which just served to accentuate the strong features of her face. Her huge blue eyes, hidden by her Jackie-O sunglasses, narrowed as she perused the scene. Leaning back in her chair, her pale skin coated with the highest-SPF sunblock she could buy, she bent one knee up, letting the flimsy material of the cover-up skirt—which really didn't cover up much at all—float around her.

Sarah reached for more sunblock, spreading it along the tender skin of her thigh, and smiled coyly at some male passersby who clearly appreciated her efforts. She didn't want a tan, but the bathing suit she wore exposed most of her skin to the sun—barring the few scraps and strings that held the thing together—so she was being careful.

Having grown up around New York City and used to northern climates, she'd just relocated to southern Virginia last August when she'd taken a new job as a computer crime investigator for the Norfolk police department. She never in her life imagined having such a perfect gig.

Up until she joined the unit, she'd been a computer hacker, making her living at various part-time jobs, though she did find occasional, profitable, under-the-table computer stints in Manhattan. It all paid the bills and allowed her to buy the gadgets she'd needed for her trade. There'd been plenty of full-time jobs available in the city, and with her skills she could have earned a decent wage on Wall Street, but that kind of work didn't satisfy her. Money wasn't her motivator; getting the bad guys was.

To that end, the larger percentage of her time had been spent in her tiny Brooklyn apartment, sitting in front of her computer tracking down Internet porn sites and clueing in the feds to what she'd found. She'd always loved the irony of breaking the law—which she'd done pretty much on a daily basis in her pursuits—to uphold it.

She had no regrets about any of the lines she had crossed in those days. The fact that she was a free agent had made her information valuable to the feds. She could go where the law couldn't—not unless they wanted Congress on their doorstep.

Hackers were a tight community, and she'd been part

of it. While she'd known people who broke the rules, most of them had been quick to help take down the real bad guys. They'd been her friends. They'd known what she was doing, though not why—and they'd never asked. But they'd helped her. And she'd helped the FBI, in turn.

That was how she'd met Ian Chandler, the FBI hotshot who'd fielded most of her information. When he quit being a fed to run his own team in Norfolk, he'd hired her as part of the unit.

Now here she was, gainfully employed doing what she was best at, earning more than enough to pay the rent and buy plenty more electronic gadgets.

Sarah gazed out over the hazy ocean horizon. She had been working constantly for six months; along with her work for the unit, she'd been attending an accelerated program at the Norfolk police academy, a requirement since she'd had no formal law enforcement training. She hadn't had a day off in a long time, and she couldn't have been happier about it. She loved her work. It was where she functioned best.

She smiled when a virile twentysomething paraded by, treating her to a view of his perfect backside adorned in skintight red neoprene surf shorts. Hey, so he was nearly a decade younger than her—she could still enjoy the view. His strong, tanned legs veed slightly as he stood in front of her talking on a cell phone. She reached down and unlaced the knot at her waist, releasing the material of her skirt altogether and bending forward to fold it neatly before leaning back.

He shifted, taking a slightly different angle—the phone not quite where he needed it to have a conversation—and her attention perked. Stretching again and letting one foot fall teasingly over the side of her chair, her toes playing in the sand. She wanted to make sure she had his attention.

She had it, all right. And him.

She waved flirtatiously, though he appeared to be looking elsewhere. He froze.

Bingo.

In the next second, he was off like a shot and Sarah was after him. He was fast, but he wasn't any match for her. At nearly six feet tall, she was all legs and she could move. She was also very, very motivated.

The hottie ran out of steam quickly and turned, panting, smiling at her engagingly.

"Hey, gorgeous."

She smiled, inclining her head in his direction. "Same backatcha."

He looked nervous. Good. He should be. She stepped a little closer, her tone friendly. "Beautiful day out here, isn't it?"

He looked around and stepped back. "Yeah. It's great."

"And yet I can't figure out why people who come to this beautiful, relaxing place would want to spend time talking on cell phones."

"Some people have business."

"And what kind of business do you have?"

She saw the flicker of panic and knew she had him. Any playfulness left her tone.

"Why don't you hand over the phone and we'll talk about the pictures you were taking of me back there?"

He grinned, though it wasn't a charming smile. "You're nuts, lady. You don't know what you're talking about."

"Really? C'mon. My guess is you got some pretty good close-ups of my boobs and crotch, but you know, it was easy—I really didn't even make you work for it."

He looked from side to side and flipped the phone nervously in his hand.

"I don't know what you're talking about. I'm going to call a lifeguard in a minute."

"Go ahead. You've been working this beach for a few weeks. I've seen the pictures that are ending up on the Web—pictures of women you've turned into your un-suspecting models—and you know, they really aren't very flattering pictures."

He stared at her for a moment, clearly unsure of what to do. Then, he threw the phone toward the surf and took off.

"Damn!"

Sarah lunged for the phone and managed to catch it midair just before it was washed over by the foamy surf splashing up on the sand. The impact knocked the wind out of her, but she was back up in a second and racing down the beach. Her body flew through the air a sec-ond time and she managed to catch him by the ankle, pulling him down hard. She winced as she felt some-thing sharp dig into her thigh, but she ignored it.

All of her attention was on maneuvering herself

around to sit on the creep's lower back, dropping down on him hard and smiling when she heard the air whoosh out of him like a deflating balloon. She planted her heel firmly at the base of his skull and pressed, ever so slightly. She looked over to see the phone lying safely in the sand, and a lifeguard running in their direction.

"What's going on here?" He looked at her bleeding leg. "You're hurt."

Her quarry started to speak, and she applied just a little more pressure with her foot, pushing his face into the sand. It was gratifying to hear him spitting in between curses. She felt the jab in her thigh again and nodded, "I think there must be some glass in the sand there—it's just a cut."

"Let me get my first aid kit, but, uh, maybe you should let that guy up?"

"Nope. He's under arrest." She smiled. "Sarah Jessup, Norfolk PD—sorry, I don't have any ID on me at the moment." She gestured to her scantily clad form. "This man is wanted for criminal activity in Norfolk and the surrounding area. I'd appreciate if you could call your local precinct for me and report this."

She rattled off the number and her badge number. "They'll confirm who I am and send someone to help me out. You can use that." She smiled, pointing to the phone lying in the sand. She enjoyed the poetic justice of using the creep's own phone to call the bust in.

The lifeguard looked a little confused, but complied, handing the phone back to her when he hung up. There was definite interest in his eyes as he took in her long limbs and flushed cheeks. He let his fingers brush hers when she took the phone, but the look she sent him told him clearly she was all business. He shrugged his tanned shoulders, heading back to his chair. Sarah poked some buttons on the phone and groaned, addressing the perp.

"Aw, man, you suck. Don't give up your day job to be a photographer. I'm nearly naked, posing for you and that's the best you could do? I mean, jeez, you're blocking the light standing there. And that is by no means my best side."

She smiled with satisfaction, clicking the phone shut and sitting back to wait for her backup. She bounced a happy little bounce on her captive's kidneys, happy to have both perp and evidence in hand.

Listening to the spits and sputters of the man she was holding immobile, she looked out at the gently rolling waves of the Atlantic as people walked by, gawking. She shrugged.

"Just doing my part for the environment, folks. Getting garbage off the beach."

A FEW HOURS later Sarah sat typing up the last of a report, reaching down every now and then to rub her thigh, which was aching like crazy now that the local anesthetic had worn off. She hated being made to go to the hospital, but she couldn't get out of it. Officer wounded on scene; it was procedure.

The six stitches she'd had to get hurt more than the initial wound, but, as she'd learned at the academy, procedure was everything. It took some getting used to, all the rules and regulations and paperwork—but it was all worth it. She loved her job.

"Hey, what happened to you?" The concerned voice that had her looking up came from one of her partners, E. J. Beaumont, known in some circles as Ethan Jared Beaumont the fourth, which she called him when she wanted to get his shorts in a knot. E.J. was the other member of their three-agent team. He wasn't alone, she noted, eyeing the beach babe standing in the doorway behind him.

"What are you doing here?"

"Forgot my cell phone last night. Came back to pick it up."

Sarah arched an eyebrow, making sure her voice was low enough for just the two of them to hear, "Looks like that's not the only thing you're picking up."

E.J. grinned, wicked mischief in his eyes. "You know, they say life is a like a box of chocolates, and I'd like to sample all I can."

Sarah laughed in spite of herself—contrary to the evidence at hand, E.J. was a real southern gentleman. Refined, intelligent and wealthy as sin, his family owned a local ship-building company. She would have expected him to be a total snob and a real bore, but he was neither.

He was a great cook, a handsome devil and a decent man. He'd given up control of his family's company to follow his heart, returning to a career in law enforcement. In the process he'd broken off his engagement with his high school sweetheart and had thrown himself headfirst into a very happy bachelorhood. Sarah wasn't sure she'd ever seen him with the same girl twice.

They'd hung out, at work and socially, keeping each other company, talking shop. At one point, he'd actually tried his charms out on her, and while she might have been the teensiest bit tempted—he was good-looking, after all—she'd shut him down. They were colleagues, and, to an extent, buddies. In a completely platonic way, she loved E.J. to death.

Then her boss, Ian, showed up in the doorway, passing a curious glance over E.J.'s "date," who fluttered her eyelashes in appreciation of Ian's dark good looks, before turning his attention to Sarah.

"Full house today. They called me about the bust, said that you got hurt. What happened? Are you okay?"

His arms were crossed over his chest, one dark eyebrow raised as he leveled a look at her that she'd gotten used to. Still, there was approval in his eyes, something she yearned for on a very basic level—the recognition of doing a good job, being believed in, making a difference.

"Yeah, I'm good." Then, in a more smartass tone, "Nice shirt, boss."

Ian looked down at the wildly patterned Hawaiian shirt that was open at the chest, and shrugged.

"Thanks. Sage bought it. She said it was "me." We're headed for the beach today. You know, to hang out, maybe cook some hot dogs. E.J., why are you here?"

"Just stopped by to get my cell phone and saw our girl working as usual."

Sarah glared at E.J., who, smiling, just popped on his

Ray-Bans, then slid his arm around his date and, with a wave, headed for the door.

Ian turned to Sarah. "I think today was a day off for you, too, right? Time to relax and leave work at the office?"

There was a not-so-subtle tone of accusation in his voice.

"Hey, I was very mellow until that idiot started taking pictures of me for his Web site. I'm sorry they called you, though. It's just a cut. I'm fine."

"No problem. I want to know when anyone is hurt. But the point is you shouldn't have been working, so I guess it was all incidental—it's not like you've been tracking him or anything like that, right? You had no idea he would be there? It just…happened?"

She knew he knew better, but she wasn't about to admit it.

"All work and no play, Sarah…" Ian shook his head.

"Would you rather I'd let him go? Have you seen that Web site? He's been at it for months, taking pictures up unsuspecting women's skirts in the park, in the mall, but the beach photos were the worst. Virginia is one of the few states that actually have active laws on up-skirting, and I intend to put them to good use."

To make sure she was getting her point across, she added, "Think about it, Ian. How would you feel if it were Sage's parts put up on the screen for the enjoyment of the general public?"

Sarah knew she'd hit a nerve when something dangerous flickered in her boss's eyes. Sage, Ian's fiancée for several months now, was the center of his life. Sage had been a convicted felon serving out a five-year prison sentence, with Ian monitoring every detail of her life for the duration. They'd gotten together when Ian had been forming the team on the request of the department. E.J. and Sarah had been Ian's backup when they'd gone after one badass computer hacker, a former lover of Sage's who'd set her up to take the fall for a computer virus he'd created and unleashed.

It had made for an odd courtship, to say the least. Sage had almost lost her life helping them catch the hacker who had victimized her. When all was said and done, though, her record had been cleared, and for the last year she'd been busy establishing her own computer security agency. In the meantime, Ian was becoming impatient waiting to make Sage his wife.

But then he smiled. "You're right, of course, but you do need to take a break. You're going to burn out."

"I feel fine."

"I've been where you are, Sarah, and I had to learn the hard way that it isn't worth it. All you do is work. You need more balance in your life."

"I like to work."

Ian glanced at the clock. "I've gotta get moving, but I'm serious. You're working way too hard—" He held his hand up to stem the objection about to pop from her lips. "You've done a great job, I'm not complaining, but I want you to take a break. I'm granting you an immediate vacation—starting Monday." He appeared to think about it for a second and spoke again, "No, starting as soon as you leave today. No work. Play only. Two weeks. It's an order."

Sarah had a hard time believing what she was hearing—he was *forcing* her to take a vacation? Wasn't that against the constitution or something?

"That's ridiculous. I don't want or need a vacation. You can't dictate my free time. I wouldn't know what to do with myself anyway, and I—"

"Exactly. That's the problem. You don't do anything but work. Sage and I went to a nice resort over in Cape Charles—it's small, more like an inn, and it's close. You can get there easily. I'll make the arrangements and all you have to do is show up on Monday. And no laptop. In fact, you can leave it here. With me." He shot her an evil grin. "And they don't allow cell phones at the resort. Or PDAs. Just so you know. If they find them, they'll ask you to store them in their office until you leave, so as not to disrupt the other guests."

Sarah felt the color drain from her face.

"No, Ian, please, I—"

"You're going. Either that or you're enrolling in the stress relief program that they're starting up this week. Make your choice."

Sarah felt her breath come up short—how *could* he? The stress relief program was a nightmare—everyone was doing whatever they could to avoid it—six weeks of deep breathing and sharing your feelings. *God.* It was a numbers game, she told herself. Two weeks of torture was better than six.

"Fine. Tell me what you want me to do, and I'll go."

Her voice was tight and unhappy, and Ian chuckled, shaking his head and turning away. "Sarah, I want you to enjoy life a little. I want you to relax, have fun. Maybe you'll even like it."

Sarah fell back in her chair, the ache in her leg throbbing more insistently as she grumbled to herself about her predicament. Vacation? No computer? No cell phone? No work?

And here she'd thought Ian liked her.

Logan Sullivan paused for a moment on the steps leading up to the broad wraparound porch that hugged the sides of the Chesapeake Inn. He felt as though he was walking into one of those old plantation-style mansions he'd seen in the movies. Colorful flowers and ivies grew everywhere, and large fig trees sprawled in the side yard. Wicker furniture was placed strategically around the large porch, some chairs grouped together if guests wanted to socialize, others tucked away in corners if they wanted to relax solo.

Not fifty yards away the Chesapeake Bay stretched out before him. The water was calm today. The Eastern Shore was a stretch of sand only a bit more than a mile wide, the Bay on one side and the ocean on the other. The little town of Cape Charles was at the southern base of the shore, its tip at the mouth of the Bay. The city of Norfolk, part of the area known as Hampton Roads, formed the other side.

Logan was familiar with the area, having lived in

Maryland his entire life. It was a marvelous place for a
vacation, and in his loose khaki shorts, white T-shirt and
worn leather sandals, he looked every bit the vacationer—which was how he wanted it. However, vacationing was the last thing on his mind.

Hefting his bags up the stairs, he opened the door and
walked in, the air-conditioning hitting him like a wave.
Though the hot weather didn't bother him at all, he still
found the coolness refreshing. And the heat here was
different, nothing like the suffocating heat he'd gotten
used to in Baltimore. Here the air was clear and a soft
breeze came in off the water, stirring the leaves on the
trees. It was pleasant.

A cheerful woman—a slim blonde who was, he
guessed, in her late fifties—rounded the corner, her face
the very definition of welcome. She reminded him a bit
of his mother, or his childhood memories of her.

"Hello! I'm Karen Sanders. You must be Mr. Sullivan.
Welcome to the Chesapeake Inn. Are these all your
bags?"

Logan smiled. It was impossible not to, her friendli-
ness made him feel at home. "No, I have more in the
car, but I'll get them. This is a gorgeous place you have.
Is this all work from local artists?" He stepped forward,
looking at some of the pencil sketches, metal sculp-
tures, and several watercolors capturing sunsets over the
Bay and other coastal scenes.

"Yes, we only feature local art, and most of these are
for sale, so let me know if there is anything you are particularly interested in. The Shore has a very interesting

and varied history, you know. There are several tours you can take, but much of the art tells the story as well."

"I'm looking forward to learning about it."

"Let me get you registered and show you to your room. We have a number of brochures that outline some tours and destinations that might interest you. We also provide equipment, kayaks and canoes, crabbing supplies and other things to keep you busy. Or you can just be quiet and relax, if that's your pleasure."

Logan nodded, knowing he would have to partake in at least some of the activities she discussed—he had to keep up appearances. Picking up his bags, he started to follow the woman past the large spiral staircase into the main room, where he could see the antique cherry registration desk, behind which was located a small office, discreetly hidden from view.

No one else was around; the other guests were probably out enjoying themselves. But before they could take more than a few steps the door opened again, and they both turned around to look.

Logan's mind went blank when he saw the woman who stepped inside. Tall, almost as tall as he was at six foot two, she was breathtaking—and strong, carrying two huge suitcases as though they were nothing. He observed the smooth, supple muscles in her upper arms and raised an eyebrow. Her short hair was a little spiky at the top, an interesting contrast that accentuated her fine, classic features.

She wore large, dark sunglasses perched on a perfectly shaped nose, so he couldn't see her eyes, but it was her mouth that fascinated him. Lipstick-free, not too full, her lips looked sweet and soft enough to eat, coming together in a natural pout that had him wetting his own lips as if in anticipation of a taste.

When their hostess moved past him to launch into her welcome routine, the woman pulled her sunglasses off and Logan was mesmerized by the bluest eyes he'd ever seen. A small smile warmed the woman's cool features as she held out her hand to the hostess.

"Hi, I'm Sarah Jessup. I'm sorry I'm here a little early, but I didn't know how long the drive would take. I hope it isn't any trouble." She looked at Logan, and then back to the hostess. "If you're busy, I can walk down to the beach or catch some lunch."

"Oh, no, no, dear, you're fine. Come on in, and we can get you and Mr. Sullivan all situated. It's nice for guests to meet each other, as you all will bump into each other during your stay. I do believe you and Mr. Sullivan are both scheduled for extended visits—two weeks, is that right?"

She looked questioningly at him, and he confirmed her claim with a short nod. The new arrival also looked back at him, then stepped forward and held out her hand.

"Well, then, hello, Mr. Sullivan. I'm Sarah."

Her voice was clear and pleasant, and he detected a strong northern accent—pure New York City. It sounded good on her. She was a tough cookie, he'd bet. And a delicious one, too. He smiled.

"Logan, please. Nice to meet you."

As he closed his hand around hers, electricity sparked between them, and Logan felt a heat invade his body that had nothing to do with the summer weather. He watched her azure eyes darken—she'd felt it, too. She dropped his hand a little abruptly and, breaking eye contact, turned back to Karen and her bags.

Intrigued, he watched the tall beauty pick up her luggage. His eyes followed the sway of her hips as she moved past him, the confident stride of her long, long legs. Logan thought he might have to make some time for fun after all.

SARAH LOOKED out the window of the quaint yellow room that she'd been shown to and admired the gardens below. A large fig tree stood beneath her window, shadowing the grass below. She licked her lips—she loved the sensual, sweet taste of figs.

Though it wasn't something she talked about much, she loved gardens. She used to spend hours walking the gorgeous pathways of the Brooklyn botanical gardens, and she'd always especially enjoyed the pockets of green among the city concrete where people grew tomatoes on stoops and had window and rooftop gardens, some of them very elaborate. Pops had had a rose garden on his patio that professionals would have envied. He used to give her roses to take home every summer; her grandfather was the only man who'd ever given her flowers.

Her bags were not unpacked yet, and she turned to open them where they lay on the large, high bed. The room was small, but light and cheerful. Ian was right, the resort was more like a bed-and-breakfast than a resort—

she had expected flashy, impersonal accommodations and crowds, bars and beaches, but this was very personal and…quiet. Maybe a little too quiet for her taste.

She wouldn't admit it to anyone but herself, especially not to Ian or anyone she worked with, but she missed the city and the beautiful borough of Brooklyn where she'd spent the past ten years. Living in Norfolk wasn't bad, but being here, where it was so slow and uncrowded, well, it made her nervous. Antsy.

The teeny apartment she'd had in the city wasn't much, a small flat on the third floor of a converted brownstone on St. Mark's Avenue, one of those built for the burgeoning working class. It was homey, though she was never much for interior decorating. But then again, she didn't need much.

She'd spent most of her time alone, and when she didn't want to be alone, she could open her window and listen to the noise on the street below. When she'd wanted company, she could sit on her stoop and chat with her neighbors, or go for a walk along Flatbush Avenue, listening to the people around her chatter in an array of languages. She'd picked up some Spanish living there, but didn't know enough to really communicate fluently.

Sometimes she'd treat herself to a Junior's cheesecake—reputed to be the best in the world—and stop by to see how old Mr. Sanchez was doing. He'd managed to hold his ground and not be pushed out of his lifelong home as building owners started renovating in order to raise rents and attract wealthier, younger Manhattanites. Just a month after she'd moved, he'd passed away from pneumonia.

She wondered who'd moved into the place now that he was gone, and a strange sense of hollowness overwhelmed her. She thought of his smile as she stared down at the fig tree, and spun away from the window, needing to get out and away from her dark thoughts.

Brochures littered the desk by one of the tall windows, things to see and do, but she walked past them. She just needed to escape for the moment. If she was going to be stuck here, she had to find something to do, but touristy activities weren't usually her thing.

True to Ian's promise, she had seen a sign when she arrived instructing guests to shut off their cell phones, and there wasn't a phone or a TV in the room—one phone and one TV were in a central room downstairs. The only computer in the place seemed to be the one the hostess had used to process reservations; otherwise it was really a low-tech operation.

She was going to get the jitters if she didn't keep herself busy. Curiously, an image of Logan popped into her mind as she walked out of her room.

2

LOGAN LAY on the sand, letting the heat soak into his skin as he forced himself to be oblivious to everything and anything as he sank into an afternoon nap. Focusing on the repetitive wash of waves rolling onto the shore, his muscles seemed to loosen, the sand cradling his body like a hug.

Naps were a luxury he almost never allowed himself, but he had to appear to be a committed vacationer. Just a guy trying to decompress from a very stressful time at work.

A shuffling in the sand interrupted his meditation and he opened his eyes to see a deliciously curved female bottom clad in the briefest of shorts, the cuffs of which graced the undersides of shapely thighs. Those were some legs. He could just make out the edge of a white bandage covering one thigh and frowned—she'd hurt herself.

It didn't stop him from admiring the feminine musculature as she braced herself in the deep sand, her bare feet planted firmly as she bent over the task of opening the beach chair that she'd apparently rented from the vendor on the sidewalk. The chair was not cooperating.

Logan helped himself to a long, leisurely view of her legs as she held the stance, smiling when she muttered something at the chair while struggling with it. He was about to offer assistance when she finally popped the contraption open, the sudden jolt of energy propelling her backward toward him.

He braced himself for impact, but she regained her balance at the last moment, though the halting action kicked sand up into his face, fortunately missing his eyes. He sputtered, wiping the grit from where it stuck to his damp skin. The beauty returned to her spot about ten feet away without so much as a second glance, sinking down into the chair, unaware she'd plastered him with sand.

He watched her stretch out and start to read, and figured the show was over. Moments after he lay back down and started to reenter that fuzzy stage of napping he'd worked hard to attain, an odd mumbling sound disturbed his concentration.

It was coming from the woman in the chair. He propped himself up on one elbow. Was she talking on a cell phone? Sitting up, curious just because, he got just close enough to hear....

"...and he laid her back, gently, as if she was the most treasured thing he'd ever had in his possession, and stared into her eyes as his long, thick hardness throbbed inside her.

"'I want all of you, Rose, and I want you to take all of me....'"

Whoa! What the heck? Then Logan realized she was reading aloud to herself, a racy novel, apparently. She wasn't speaking loudly, but in a soft, throaty mumble that certainly made *him* want to hear more. He leaned in and listened a little more closely.

"'Please, Russell…I love you. I need you. I need…more!'"

Russell? Russell and Rose? Logan quirked a grin. This was pretty good.

"She tightened around him, waves of pleasure crashing through her though she tried to hold back, but Russell wouldn't let her. He thrust himself into her, pushing red-hot pleasure through her like a sword that pierced her completely and took her breath away—"

"Okay, now that just doesn't sound like fun."

He didn't realize the comment had actually come out of his mouth until the sexy mumbling ceased. The woman swung her incredible legs over the side of the chair, peering at him over the same stylish sunglasses she'd been wearing earlier that day when he'd met her by the door of the inn. He hadn't recognized her from the rear view, nice as it had been.

"Pardon me?" The sexy whisper she'd been reading in shifted to a cool interrogative, and he cleared his throat. There was something about when a woman peered over the top of her glasses that was so totally sexy and completely intimidating. Especially when paired with the high cheekbones and those amazingly shaped lips. She caught his gaze and held it. Not that *he* was intimidated, even though her tone remained cool and challenging.

"You have an opinion you'd like to share?"

He smiled in what he hoped was a friendly and charming manner. "I thought the whole sword piercing thing didn't sound very…romantic. Or pleasurable. I wouldn't want a woman to feel like that when I was, uh. You know."

A delicate eyebrow raised, and her head cocked sideways as she blinked at him.

"When you were…what?" Her tone was innocent, but suddenly he felt like a mouse being batted around the kitchen floor by a cat. He leaned in a little more closely, softening his own tone, meeting the challenge.

"When my thick, throbbing hardness is buried inside of her."

He'd give her credit; she didn't even blink and didn't back down. She looked back down at her book, studying it for a moment, then looked back at him.

"Actually, it was his long, thick hardness throbbing inside of her."

"Sorry, you'll have to speak up a little more next time, so I get it right."

"Maybe you should be minding your own business."

"Hey, you were reading out loud—Sarah, was it?"

"Still is."

"Well, I was sleeping, but you kicked sand in my face

when you stumbled back from that chair, and you've interrupted my nap—twice. I couldn't help but listen in,
you were reading aloud for everyone to hear, and since
I couldn't sleep..." His words were accusatory, but his
tone wasn't, and her smile twitched then widened as she
shook her head, giving in.

"Sorry. I didn't realize you could hear me. When
I pulled up you looked dead to the world. I would
have sat farther away, but I really wanted to find a spot
that was out of the way of the action." She looked out
at the busy beach, her beautiful blue eyes drifting
over the children playing and a group of teens playing volleyball.

"No problem. What are you reading?"

"A book I found in the room."

"You like romances?"

She shrugged. "Sometimes. I like romantic sus-
pense more than this kind of thing. This is pretty bor-
ing, really."

"Even with all the sword-piercing pleasure and such?"

She smiled again, looking at him fleetingly then
turning her gaze toward the water of the Bay. He
sensed that she wasn't really seeing him or any of the
beautiful scenery around her. She'd retreated, and he
could feel the distance between them in her next
words.

"I'm sorry I disturbed you." She started to swing her
legs back over the chair, but he didn't want to let her go
just yet.

"Why do you read out loud like that?"

She looked back, obviously wishing she'd been able to succeed with her abrupt dismissal, but then stopped and shrugged.

"I spend a lot of time in front of a computer. Sometimes the surroundings are noisy, so I read out loud while I work, it makes it easier to concentrate. I guess it just got to be a habit. I never really noticed."

"That makes sense."

She tipped her sunglasses back up on her face, fully covering her eyes. "Sorry again for bothering you."

"No problem."

When he lay back on his towel, all he could hear was the slosh of the waves and the voices of the volleyball players. He almost asked her to start reading again.

SARAH HELD her book in front of her face, but she couldn't concentrate on Rose and Russell's antics anymore, not that she had been all that into it in the first place. The sex being described on the page had heated up considerably when the man behind her had decided to share his opinion on what a woman felt when a man was inside her.

It was something Sarah tried not to think about too often. She knew *a lot* about sex, more than she wanted to. She was exposed to the seedier side of it as part of her job, and suffice it to say it was nothing like what Rose and Russell were experiencing.

She snorted softly to herself. Nothing about sex was like what Rose and Russell were experiencing. Sex could be fun and relaxing at best, and as for the worst, well, she wouldn't go there. She saw too much of it in her work. Her job allowed her to think she'd made a difference in the world, but along the way, she knew something inside her had been irrevocably lost.

That sense of loss, combined with scars from her past, had left her sleeping alone for several years now. She'd gotten used to it and even preferred it; she knew how to take the edge off when she really needed to. Men were an unnecessary complication, and sometimes a dangerous one.

So why, when the gorgeous man sleeping on the sand behind her had looked at her in just that particular, teasing way, and had offered her a smile that made her toes dig down in the sand, had she not shut him down as hard as she usually did? Why had she talked with him—even flirted a little—and felt a...*tug?* She wanted no part of tugs.

Tugs led to pulls, and pulls led to grasping, which inevitably led to sliding, pushing, rubbing and thrusting—*ahhhh!*

She threw the book down on the sand, disgusted and appalled that just thinking about it had her nipples poking through her tank top and her thighs flexing slightly in response to her unwanted desire.

This was totally out of character. She wanted to kill Ian for sending her on this vacation.

"It sucks that bad, huh?"

And sucking. Yes, tugs could lead to sucking, too. And licking.... *Oh, damn, just stop already!*

Sarah drew a deep breath. Logan had spoken to her again, but she was determined to just ignore him this time.

"I thought you were napping."

So much for ignoring him.

Vacation was obviously playing havoc with her normal sense of independence and self-control.

"I couldn't get back to sleep. I was too worried about what was happening with Rose and Russell."

She wanted to laugh and had to choke it down.

"The usual. Piercing and poking and such."

"Sounds painful."

"Some people are into that."

"Are you?" The question was baldly stated and openly curious. He was flirting with her. Well, she would put an end to it.

"No."

She rose, struggling with the stupid beach chair once again. The stupid joints wouldn't bend, corroded by salt or age or something, and she grimaced, putting as much muscle into it as possible. The chair gave way, the metal bending under the force of her efforts, the joints popping altogether.

"Ouch. You sure wrestled that into submission."

Didn't this guy ever quit? Still, something about his light, teasing tone and comment broke through her annoyance, and she shook her head, chuckling lightly.

"It really wasn't a fair fight."

"Understandable. The chair is clearly an unworthy opponent."

Was he suggesting that he would be worthy? She stood, picking up the broken chair, looking down at Logan and feeling that stupid, aggravating tug yet again.

Okay, so he *was* eye candy. Lean and tall, he lay over the sand with the kind of reckless sexuality that probably made women turn to jelly with just a glance, though he didn't seem to be posing. He wasn't leering or posturing, he was just…lying there.

His lean legs stretched out before him, feet half-buried in the sand. The light scattering of dark hair over his legs continued upward, gathering into a light seam over his flat stomach that thickened a bit on his chest. He had strong shoulders and tight, well-shaped arms. Nice chin, good cheekbones. Firm lips. He was what she'd always thought of as "whiplike"—thin and sinewy, stronger than someone might assume at first glance. Probably fast.

There was a straight, white scar on his shoulder, about two inches long, and she almost asked him where it came from when she realized she'd been staring.

Damn. When caught, pretend not to notice, and then run as fast as you can.

He was looking up at her silently, waiting for her to finish her obvious inspection. He wasn't the outdoorsy type, she guessed. His skin was not quite as light as hers, but it was clear he wasn't used to being out in the sun.

"You're going to burn if you stay out here much longer."

With that clipped statement, she turned and walked toward the sidewalk.

She hadn't made it halfway across the beach when she realized he'd caught up and was walking beside her. He stood just a little taller than she did, which meant he was at least six foot, maybe a little more, since she came in at five-ten in bare feet. When his arm brushed up against hers, she subtly stepped to the side as she kept walking, not wanting the contact.

"I'll vouch for you that the chair broke when you sat in it and let the vendor know he should be lucky if you don't sue him."

"It didn't break when I sat in it."

"Just trying to save you an argument."

She slid him a sidelong glance. "He won't argue with me."

A moment of silence as he digested that.

"Where are you from?"

"Brooklyn." Regardless of where she lived now, or where she was born, she would always be from Brooklyn.

"Really? Your accent is certainly that of a New Yorker, but I wouldn't have guessed Brooklyn."

"I don't have an accent."

"Okay. Right. So what do you do in Brooklyn?"

He was not going to be easy to discourage. She looked at him through her shades, knowing he couldn't see her eyes. She wasn't really annoyed with him, she was irritated with her entire situation at the moment. She let that fuel her tone as she shut him down, once and for all.

"Listen, slick, thanks for the conversation but I'm not interested, okay? Have a nice nap."

Turning to walk away, she didn't look back as she left him standing quietly behind her.

LOGAN STOOD on the sand and felt put in his place, good and proper. Granted, he hadn't dated in a while, and his social skills were probably a little rusty, but...*ouch*. And given the classic male sense of the hunt, wanting to go after things that presented a challenge, he was even more interested now.

He watched her hand the chair to the sidewalk vendor, who appeared to be apologizing profusely, his eyes level with her breasts the whole time he spoke. Sarah put one hand on a cocked hip and shot the other one to the guy's chin, nudging his eyes up to meet hers. Whatever she said to him had those shocked eyes widening and he nodded quickly, handing her money back and not letting his gaze dip south again.

Logan smiled widely to no one in particular. It was clear Sarah was a woman who could take care of herself and who didn't suffer fools lightly.

She'd shut him down, but he hadn't mistaken her slight flirtation with him earlier, when he'd caught her reading. And even as she told him to pack sand, so to speak, her nipples budded endearingly against the soft material of the tank she wore.

Was she as interested as he was? He felt a curl of heat in his belly and knew he wanted to find out. He was male, she was gorgeous and he was on vacation, right?

Normal physical desire, effectively erased by the enormous stress he'd been under, suddenly thrummed through his bloodstream again when he pictured Sarah's mouth. He could imagine kissing her, tasting her, and let himself imagine her wrapping those lips around him in the most intimate way....

He dropped back to his towel just in time to stretch

out on his side lest anyone notice the somewhat un-
timely erection that sprang to life in response to his
thoughts. He was reacting like a horny teenager, but he
didn't really mind, though true, it was inconvenient to
be sitting here in public with a boner. It took him by surprise that he wanted her so distinctly. He took a deep
breath to calm down and reminded himself why he was
really here.

Finding out what had happened to Melanie, his partner for eight years on the Baltimore police force, that
was his goal. Mel had had some problems, sure—especially right before she'd disappeared, she'd been on a
disciplinary office suspension after having a few too
many one night while on duty. She'd been dumped by
her fiancé. And shortly after that, she'd had a violent en-
counter in an alley, as well. Both had left her nerves
frayed, and her normally sound sense of judgment
weakened by self-doubt. But she was a good cop, and
a good partner. Logan believed that then, and he still believed it.

She'd thrown the suspension back in their faces, taking vacation time and heading to Virginia Beach. It was
the last anyone had seen of her until some ugly photographs had surfaced during another investigation—ex-
plicit, pornographic footage in which Mel was clearly
the star.

The department was concerned about its public
image, but they also considered her trouble waiting to
happen, and no one seemed to surprised she'd gone off
the deep end and gotten involved with a bad crowd. A

really bad crowd, by the looks of it. Though they'd made the appearance of an investigation, there was no concern about foul play, since she was obviously alive in the photos, and they hadn't taken too seriously the fact that no one had heard from her in three months. That was six months ago, almost to the day, and though it seemed logical that she wouldn't want to stay in contact with her friends and family, Logan's gut told him there was more to it, and he couldn't let it go.

He couldn't drop it, though he'd been warned to do so. He knew Melanie, had spent hours every day with her, seen her put her life on the line just like every other cop did. She wouldn't have just dropped everything to leave town and pick up a gig as a nude model—a polite description of what the pictures illustrated—even if she was going through a really rough patch. Something was very wrong, but he couldn't seem to convince anyone else of that. He needed evidence.

So he'd made it his personal mission to find her again, or at least to find out what had happened to her. Doing so had taken over his life, interfered with his work, though he'd tried to keep his investigation low-key. He wasn't in love with Mel, but she'd been a good cop and deserved better than she was getting.

She'd been a close friend; he'd met her family. He'd eaten dinner with her parents. And he knew firsthand what it was like to lose people who were close to you, what it was like to lose family. How could he face her family or tell them he'd given up?

The trail had led him here. But he had to be smart

about it, because he'd been ordered to take a mandatory leave when he'd tried to make his case to the captain, to show him the new leads he'd found. When they'd refused to budge and turned their backs he'd lost it completely, blowing up in front of everyone in the captain's office.

His job was on the line, but he wasn't going to let it go. He had to make sure it looked like he was having a genuine vacation. He didn't think anyone was watching him—he wasn't that important—but he'd rather be safe than sorry.

And how better to do that than to engage in a vacation fling with a beautiful woman? As a cover, it had numerous advantages.

He pictured Sarah in his mind's eye and smiled. He wouldn't be working every minute, and maybe she would provide the perfect distraction. She wasn't going to be easily convinced, but then, he'd always enjoyed the hunt.

SARAH WAS still mumbling to herself as she pushed her key into the lock on the door of her room and froze, finding it open. Someone was inside.

She pushed the door open a little more with her fingertip, silently, slowly, holding her breath until she had it open far enough that she could see inside, though part of the room was blocked from view.

She heard humming, and frowned. Someone sounded pretty happy in there. Definitely a female voice. She was relieved she didn't have anything with her worth stealing. She'd left all of her computer equipment back in Norfolk. Ian's orders, damn him. But she still didn't like the idea of anyone going through her stuff.

A young woman moved into her line of vision. She was pulling some faded flowers out of the vase by the window and replacing them with fresh ones. Not exactly burglar behavior. Sarah pushed the door open and stepped inside, sighting a small service cart she hadn't spotted from the crack in the door.

The maid.

She sighed heavily, feeling the tension drain away, irritation returning. She hadn't spent much time in hotels or inns, and hadn't even considered that there would be a maid in her room. She hadn't even slept in the room yet, what was there to clean up?

Her suspicions suddenly seemed silly, even to her. It wasn't like the small, quaint town of Cape Charles was a hotbed of crime—they left the door to the main house open all day, even when no one was around. Sarah couldn't quite get used to that fact. Her suspicions were misplaced, the result of city living and the extreme boredom she was experiencing at the moment.

The young woman turned, smiling, and that smile faded suddenly. Sarah experienced a pinch of guilt as she realized she was standing there scowling at the girl for no good reason. She could feel her cheeks all bunched up. She tried to relax, though she couldn't quite manage a smile. The maid wrung her hands, apparently feeling caught in the act even though she obviously hadn't been doing anything wrong. Sarah felt like a jerk.

"I-I'm sorry, we try to be out of the rooms before—"

"It's okay. You just startled me." At the girl's doubtful glance, she reiterated, "Really. Thanks for freshening the flowers." Sarah didn't know what else to say—was she supposed to tip her or something?

"You're welcome. I'll just get out of your way now." The young woman rolled the small cart to the door and stopped. "Thanks for not being angry. I really need this job in the summer to save money for college. But we're supposed to be out of the rooms when guests are around. It's just that I forgot to change your flowers this morning, and figured I could stop back and—"

"It's okay. What's your name?"

The girl blanched, and Sarah realized she probably thought she was going to be reported.

"Ivy."

Sarah smiled, trying to prove she wasn't the wicked witch of the east. "Thanks, Ivy. And don't worry about getting in here while I'm not around. After a few more days of this, I'll need the company."

"What do you mean?"

Sarah sighed, sitting on the bed, waving her hand around aimlessly. "I'm not used to…this. There's nothing to do, no one around."

"You don't like the quiet? It's why most people come here."

"Not me. My boss is an ass—uh, idiot who thought I needed a break and he made the reservations for me. He thought I was wound a little too tightly and needed to relax."

Ivy kept quiet, her fingers poised on the doorknob, and Sarah felt the need to clarify.

"I just like my work is all. I don't get burnt out. He doesn't seem to get that."

"What do you do? Are you a model?"

Sarah blinked, surprised. She knew she wasn't ugly, but she'd never thought of herself as model material.

"Oh, no way. I'm a cop."

She almost smiled as Ivy's eyes widened in surprise. "A cop? Like, a real one? A detective like on *CSI?*"

"Not like that, but I work in a special unit with the Norfolk police department."

"Do you have a gun?"

"Yeah, but not here."

"That is so cool. You are so pretty. I never would've guessed you're a cop."

Sarah felt inordinately pleased by the compliment, and shrugged. "Thanks. It's kind of a new job, actually, so I didn't really need this vacation. I'm going to go slowly insane if I don't find some way to pass the time. I'm here for two weeks, and I just can't sit around on the beach all day. And there's no shopping here. Or anything."

Frustration edged itself into her tone again, but this time Ivy seemed to understand.

"Well, it is peaceful here. Most people come here to get away from all that, from the noise and stuff. But there is a lot to do."

"Like what?"

"Do you like crabbing?"

"I don't like complainy people—"

Ivy laughed. "No, I mean, like getting crabs, to eat. You can do your own crabbing."

Sarah just raised her eyebrows. The closest she'd ever come to getting her own live seafood was buying it at street markets in New York.

"Anything else?"

"Well, there are some museums and historic stops. Assateague and Chincoteague aren't far away. You can see the wild horses and deer there on the beaches, which are incredible. Or, oh, you can take a kayak lesson with Jim McIntyre, he gives a discount to resort guests, and he's like a magician on the water."

Ivy's cheeks had stained a light pink as she spoke about the kayak instructor, and Sarah guessed the young woman had a little more interest in him than a business referral.

"Is he your boyfriend?"

Pink turned to full-out red, and Ivy shook her head vehemently.

"No, no." She sounded very disappointed by this fact. "But I wouldn't say he's the best just because of that. He really is very good."

"And you like him? For more than his ability as a kayak instructor?"

Ivy hesitated, biting her lip, then nodded.

"Have you told him?"

"No. I couldn't do that."

"Why not?"

"He's a little older."

"How much older?"

"Twenty-six."

"And you're…?"

"Just twenty."

Sarah took a deep breath. Numerically that wasn't a huge difference, but she was willing to bet that in terms of experience, it was. By the way she was blushing, Sarah would lay odds that Ivy was as pure as the spotless white sheets she'd just put on the bed.

"Well, it's probably just as well. Men can be more trouble than they're worth."

A small crease appeared on Ivy's smooth brow in response to her statement. "Really? I bet you have guys asking you out all the time."

Sarah shook her head. "Not really. I guess they pick up on the vibe that I give out."

"A cop vibe? They don't like that?"

"I don't know if it's that, but you have to be careful about men, Ivy. What you see is almost never what you get. And what you get is often a whole pack of trouble."

Ivy seemed to have a hard time digesting that. "I should get going. I have to finish up. It was nice talking to you. Thanks for not being mad, you know, about the room."

"Anytime. I hope we get to chat again. And don't worry about this Jim guy. You're probably too good for him anyway."

Ivy smiled and closed the door, and Sarah lay back on the bed, feeling a little less irritated after talking with Ivy. The day hadn't been a total waste after all; at least she'd been able to give some decent advice to the younger woman. Sarah wished someone had made certain things about men clear to her before she'd made some of the biggest mistakes of her life. If she could save girls like Ivy some of that pain, it was worth it.

3

LOGAN DIDN'T so much as move to rub his eyes, even though they stung from the bright blue light of the laptop screen that held his attention. The satellite Internet service that the inn used had been difficult to tap into. It was slow, and if it happened to be rainy or cloudy, he could forget it, but he'd lucked out tonight. The weather was clear, and every star in the southeastern sky was out—not that he was stargazing.

In fact, what he was looking at was far less pleasant. He'd discovered where Mel's pictures had been posted from and after doing more investigating he'd found two other women from the same porn site who'd been reported as missing. They were from different cities, but they'd all vacationed in the same place, Virginia Beach.

It was the link he had been looking for. If his somewhat lacking computer skills and the computer connection he'd wired up would hold, maybe he could find those final pieces of the puzzle even sooner than he'd hoped.

He'd wanted to go to the same hotel Mel had stayed at, but that would have looked too suspicious. So he'd made some phone calls and had asked her family and friends to see if they knew more about her vacation plans, had received postcards, or anything of the sort.

He'd finally hit pay dirt—Mel's best friend, a chatty woman named Terri, had told him that Mel had met some guy and had been excited about going on an offshore gambling boat. Apparently, the man she'd hooked up with was a high roller looking for eye candy, and Mel had been vulnerable after her breakup. Maybe the man was the one who could explain what had happened to Mel. Logan had tried to get a description, but Terri hadn't had too many details.

Logan had an itch that this was the lead he needed. He'd heard of offshore gaming, operations where tourists were taken far enough out to sea that federal and state laws about gambling—and God knows what else—didn't apply.

It was a popular business, and lots of tourists took advantage, not always aware of what they were getting into. Unregulated, many of the boats that promoted offshore gaming were suspected of being involved in the drug trade, as well as money laundering. So it was more than possible that one of them could be running a pornography operation on the side. And the Internet was the perfect vehicle to distribute their product, since the boats frequently offered online gambling.

Logan needed passenger lists and schedules, and he had to find out which boat Mel had been on. Clenching his jaw over the slow response of his connection, he waited, determined to be patient as he downloaded everything he could find about local tours available, their routes and schedules.

He didn't have any proof yet, but his gut told him that he was on the right track.

SARAH FOUND herself wandering around aimlessly later that evening. She'd fallen asleep after Ivy had left, and though she'd had only a restless nap, she'd gotten up past dinnertime and was now completely awake with nothing to do. It was nearing nine o'clock and almost dark. She was hungry, and thought she would go and find some food. After a brief venture outside, she'd quickly slipped back in the door after being swarmed by mosquitoes.

Great. Just wonderful.

She poked around the downstairs of the inn, chatting with some of the guests, but most of them were couples who retired to their rooms shortly after she appeared.

Plopping down into a deep leather sofa in the main room, her spirits really plummeted when she realized that the TV offered only local channels, and local channels had next to nothing on. She really was in hell. If she hadn't been stressed out before her vacation started, she would be by the time she got home.

She disliked being at loose ends, at night most of all. The daylight drove away most of her demons, but in the lonely hours of the evening, she usually had to work to keep her thoughts from eating her alive. Her mother used to caution that idle hands did the devil's work. For the most part she'd left her devils firmly in the past; but at night, if it was too quiet, when the loneliness took over they still haunted her.

Crossing the room to the registration desk, she heard some murmuring coming from a small room to the back. Curious and looking for anything to do, anyone to talk to, she went in the direction of the voice.

An older man sat at a computer, swearing profusely under his breath. She recognized him; he was Harold Sanders, Karen's husband. Harold was a polite and polished guy, and here he was swearing like a sailor. Computers brought out that familiar stream of colorful language in the best of people. He appeared to be at the end of his rope.

Sarah knocked softly, and he managed a small, polite smile when he saw her in the doorway.

"Yes, um, Ms. Jessup. I'm sorry, I didn't hear you—is there something you need?"

Sarah wasn't sure what to say. Directing her eyes to the computer he sat in front of, hoping she didn't look like an addict in desperate need of a fix, she tried to sound casual.

"Having computer problems?"

Harold emitted a gusty sigh. "I'm sorry. I must have been turning the air blue, eh?" He settled back in his seat, gesturing in disgust toward the desktop computer.

"This satellite connection we have usually works pretty well. Sometimes it's slow, but no worse than your average modem, and it's usually enough for our needs. Tonight something is bogging it down, and I don't understand it—I'm not handling any huge files, and the weather is clear."

Sarah nodded. "Want me to take a look?"

Harold looked at her doubtfully. "You know anything about these things?"

"A bit. It's my work. I don't know what I can do, but
I could probably tell you if it's a problem with your machine or your network—you might have a virus."

He looked hesitant. "Oh, I hope not. I keep the virus
detection software updated. But I don't think I should
have you working on your vacation—Karen would have
a fit."

Sarah smiled sweetly, trying not to appear too eager.
Maybe if she could look at his machine, she might be
able to sneak in a look at her e-mail, her discussion
groups…just one little peek.

"No problem at all. Truth is, I was kind of restless
and at loose ends, wandering around when I found you.
You'd be doing me a favor if you let me have a look at
it."

His brow creased in concern. "You're not enjoying
your stay?"

She hedged, realizing she was on delicate ground.
"It's my first day—you know how it takes some time to
adjust to a new place, a new schedule. It's beautiful
here, but I'm just not in vacation mode yet."

"I understand. It can be hard to wind down if you're
used to a busy schedule."

She looked expectantly at the computer, then stepped
forward when he was still hesitant. "It should only take
me a few minutes. Why don't you get something to drink?
I…I could use something as well. It's so hot tonight."

Harold, looking relieved that he had a way to both

escape his problem and serve his guest, stood up quickly, surrendering his chair.

Sarah sat down, running her fingers over the keyboard like a caress, a calm focus overcoming her as she tapped keys and studied the lines of text flying over the black background of the DOS box she'd called up.

Harold set an icy glass of tea by the side of the monitor, and she addressed him without looking up.

"Do you share this connection with any other computer in the inn or another business?"

"No, this is the only machine, and we just have one account on the connection. As you know, laptops and other such things are discouraged here. They interrupt the vacation environment."

Sarah choked down a scoff. "Yes, well, as far as I can tell, you have someone sucking bandwidth off your connection."

"I'm sorry…?"

"Someone is tapping into your connection. It seems like it would have to be someone physically here, in the building, but it could be a neighbor or someone nearby. Wireless and satellite connections are easy for others to tap into, much like splicing a television cable connection, if you know how to do it."

Harold seemed at a loss. "But who would do such a thing? We know all of our neighbors. They wouldn't— are you sure that's what it is?"

His tone turned skeptical, perhaps unconvinced that a woman could make this technical assessment, she thought sourly. She'd run into that problem before, when she'd tried white collar work, where it was more important to her IT colleagues that she was datable than if she was competent. At least her little hacker circles had been a level playing field.

"I'm sure. It would be hard for me to explain to you why, but it's there, believe me. I do this kind of thing every day. With some more work, I can probably trace the machine, maybe get the user's name, but probably not the location."

"And you know how to do this?"

"Like I said, it's part of my job."

"Yes, well, this is all very disturbing. You can't find who it is? Have they, uh, hacked into our machine?"

Sarah shook her head. "They're using your connection, but your machine seems fine. The only way I could find out who they are—maybe—is if I got into their machine and could track down some identifying information."

She caught Harold's startled glance and sat back, grabbing her tea. "But that wouldn't really be legal, or necessary. However, I *can* cause them a little inconvenience." Sarah smiled slyly, catching Harold's eye. "I can shut them out. They may find a way back in, but for now they'd be locked out, and you would have your connection back and running faster. You can report the breach to your satellite provider tomorrow, and see what they can do to prevent it from happening again."

Relief brightened her host's features. "That sounds wonderful. Would you like a snack with your tea? Karen made pie earlier."

"Harold, you are a man after my own heart."

She smiled with sheer joy. Hacking and snacking—exactly what she'd needed to feel like herself again, and to have some fun.

Shutting off the interloper wasn't exactly easy, but she knew she could get in there and do it, given a few minutes. Grinning, she imagined the hacker's frustration when his or her connection was cut. Probably a neighborhood teen who'd figured out how to jump on the wireless connection for a free ride. No doubt as bored and restless as she was.

When she was done, she'd also warn Harold about handing over his computer to a strange user so easily, and run him through the basics of security, both human and technical. If she were a corrupt person, she could get control of their network, or get enough informationto do the small resort some serious damage. Hackers took exactly these kinds of opportunities to do their thing, sometimes right underneath people's noses.

Forgetting that, she became so caught up in her work, she barely noticed anything, mumbling to herself and lost in the world of codes and programs, completely forgetting about Harold until she heard him snoring lightly, and looked over to see the older man had fallen asleep in a chair. His thin, gold, wire-frame glasses slid down his nose a little bit, and she felt affection for him, even though she didn't know him very well.

Sleeping like that, he reminded her of her grandfather, and the memory brought both a smile and an ache. Pops was gone now, and she missed him horribly. He'd been the only one in her family who hadn't judged her harshly for her mistakes.

Sighing, she decided against checking her e-mail or lists—for all she knew, Ian or E.J. had put a sniffer out there to tag her if she showed up, and Ian would dock her vacation pay if he caught her, as he'd threatened before she left. She finished off the fantastic banana cream pie Harold had brought her and shut the screen down.

Closing up shop, she reassured herself that the problem was solved for the moment. Pulling his jacket from the back of his chair, she covered Harold up and left him a quick note, whispering the words out loud as she wrote them. *Harry, Connection fixed. Thanks for the snack. S.J.*

Wandering back up the stairs, she grabbed a bunch of magazines from a stack on a table and grimaced as she glanced at the titles: *Country Living, Martha Stewart Living* and *Sport Fisherman.*

No *Cosmo, People* or, better yet, techie mags like *2600* or *Secure Enterprise.* Even *Wired* would do in a pinch. Ah, well, beggars couldn't be choosers and it was going to be a long night. She could have gone several more hours online before winding down, and now she had a buzz from her light hacking episode. She grinned, the familiar happiness gripping her whenever she thought about the fact that she was *paid* to do this kind of work now.

As she reached the top landing, another door softly shut. Not really paying attention, she kept walking and nearly collided head-on with Logan—a noticeably more tense Logan than she had met that afternoon. He looked like something had really pissed him off.

She felt another, stronger tug. She liked him looking this way, and she could feel the energy that practically arced through the air like an electrical current. She took in the tight black T-shirt that hugged his firm upper body, and the worn jeans, feeling that surge of interest again.

"You okay?"

His eyes snapped toward her and he stepped back, running a hand through already disheveled ebony hair, getting control of himself.

"Yeah, just restless, and hot—did the AC break? I'm heading out for a beer."

She stared at him—the inn was kept at a comfortable seventy degrees, but he did look overly warm.

"Want company?"

They were both surprised at her question, but she didn't take it back—she didn't have anything better to do.

"Sure."

Shrugging, she did an about-face and headed back down the stairs in front of him. At the bottom, she put the magazines back.

"You know anywhere to go?"

"I spotted a small place in town this morning, on my way in. I hope it's still open. It's within walking distance."

"Everything is," she replied with light sarcasm. "The mosquitoes will carry us back and forth. It's bad out there, take it from me. I can drive." She hesitated at the door, wanting to get out, but not relishing all the itchy bites that awaited her. Logan pursed his lips thoughtfully.

"Hold on."

As she watched him disappear past the kitchen, she wondered what he was up to. He returned a few minutes later holding a small, green aerosol can.

"Heavy-duty stuff. It smells, and you should shower it off so it's not on your skin all night, but it'll do the job for now."

Sarah grinned and held out her arms. "Do me."

No sooner were the words spoken than she felt the clog in her throat, and he slanted her a roguish smile, the tension in his face easing as he pointed the can at her.

"Your wish is my pleasure."

Sarah closed her eyes as he covered her lightly with spray and wrinkled her nose as the strong scent surrounded them and she felt the cool aerosol on her skin. He did both legs and then moved up her torso and by the time he got to her arms, she was tingling all over. It shouldn't have been sexy, but…

"Hold out your hands."

She opened her eyes. "Why?"

"You can rub it on your neck and over your hair without getting it on your face."

She frowned, placing her hands palms up. "This is ridiculous. I feel like I'm going on safari, not for a beer."

"Small price to pay. You should wash your hands before we go, too."

She put her hand out for the can. "Your turn."

"I can get myself."

She shrugged. "It's your skin, slick."

She walked back and washed her hands quickly before rejoining him. The entire lobby smelled like bug spray, but they were done and out the door, walking into the heavy, humid night air. Mosquitoes buzzed around them, disappointed and not biting. Sarah smiled.

"I'm glad you found that spray. I was going nuts in there."

"Having a hard time settling into vacation?"

"Yeah, I guess."

"Me, too. It's been a while."

"I guess you have to ease into it. Vacation can be hard work."

They continued the pleasant small talk as they walked the narrow town streets toward the main strip, where they found the bar was still open. There were a few people around, touring the street that looked out over the marinas and the harbor, and the Coast Guard station buzzed with activity just across the way.

The bar was small, quiet and bathed in golden light. Sarah was surprised to see a small band setting up in the corner. Live music—who would've thought? Small wooden tables were scattered everywhere, and Logan led her to one near a dusky corner, away from the band.

They gave the waitress their orders and faced each other quietly in the dim light. Strangers sitting together like old friends, waiting for a beer. It was intimate, uncomfortably so. Sarah shifted in her chair, looking at the handsome man who sat so close to her that their knees almost touched under the small table. She moved hers to the left, trying to discreetly avoid the contact, and smiled at the young waitress when she delivered two frosty beers to the table.

"So…"

"So…"

They spoke simultaneously, laughed together, and broke the strain somewhat. Logan lifted his beer to her, and she did the same before drinking.

"It's a shame."

"What's that?" Tilting her beer back, she took a sip, letting the amber liquid slide down her throat. It was perfect.

"The two of us, apparently such workaholics that we can't get into the vacation groove." He smiled across the table, tipping his bottle toward her. "But I have to admit, things are looking up."

Sarah smiled and took another swig, trying to decide how to respond. She didn't want to invite anything inadvertently—or did she? No. She didn't know him, didn't know what kind of man he was. You could never trust the impressions people offered you.

Swallowing slowly, she met his gaze, and found nothing more than friendly interest there. She loosened up.

"I've never had an actual vacation, not since I was a kid. I guess I don't know what to do with myself."

"Who do you work for? They don't offer any vacation time?"

"Oh, no. They offer it, but I don't take it." She began to explain further and then changed her mind. For some reason, she didn't want to talk with him about her job. "Let's not talk about work. Maybe we can help each other get into this vacation groove."

His eyes warmed and she watched as the rim of the

bottle was held poised before his straight, firm and slightly wet lips. Uh-oh.

"Fair enough. Let's start over. No work, just play. Sound good?"

She nodded, oddly relieved.

"I wonder what kind of music they're going to have." He glanced toward the band, and then looked back to her.

"I just hope it's not country. That really would be the last straw."

As if by magic, two more beers appeared on the table, and Sarah realized she was feeling a little woozy. She had missed dinner, and the beer, which normally didn't have more effect on her than a carbonated drink, was fuzzing her brain.

"I could use something to eat. Do they have a menu?"

A short time later, more beers were delivered, along with a stack of wings and loaded potato skins. Sarah gazed at the food adoringly and loaded up her plate.

"Ah, heaven."

Logan watched her eat with a combination of admiration and humor, helping himself as well. Sarah seemed to have forgotten him altogether as she concentrated on the food, a slight flush coloring the fine skin of her cheekbones, a little bit of sauce from a wing clinging to her jaw. He reached over, swiping it away with his finger.

"I like a woman with healthy appetites."

Heat sparked between them, and Logan didn't know if it was the lateness of the hour, or the beer, or both. He didn't care. Sarah was gorgeous, even stuffing her face with wings. He smiled when she sat back, sated.

"So, we can't talk about work, but we can talk about other stuff. Get to know each other a little better."

"Like what?" She frowned, wondering what he wanted to know, though in all honesty she was curious about him, too.

"Well…" He grinned in the direction of the band, definitely of the country-rock variety. "You apparently don't like country music. What kind do you like?"

This was a safe enough topic. "I visit a lot of jazz clubs and alternative music spots in the city. Some punk, techno—that kind of thing. It's where a lot of my friends hang out." She decided to keep things in the present tense—she'd told him before she was from Brooklyn, and there wasn't any reason to complicate things now. And she couldn't explain her move without explaining her job. Depending on what was happening here, maybe it was best he believed she lived back up north.

"They're musicians?"

"Some."

"Techno, huh? Do you ever rave?" he asked with a smile and she smiled back.

"I've been once or twice. It's a little too crazy for me, and I prefer to keep my mind and body clean. Drugs aren't a requirement, of course, but they're pretty prevalent in the clubs. Not my scene, really."

"Me, either. But it sounds like an exciting life."

"Not especially." She smiled, thinking of the movie portrayals of hackers, all dressed in black with slick haircuts and shiny earrings, attending raves every night and talking the talk.

Some of that was true—there was a distinct "look" among her old set of friends—but the lifestyle wasn't really all that glamorous or exciting. Sitting in front of a computer for hours—or days—on end wasn't the stuff excitement was made of. Not unless you were into it.

"It's just a life." She took a swig of beer, looking at him over the top of the bottle. "So what about you?"

He shrugged. "I like most music, nothing in particular though. I go to outdoor concerts back home, but I have never really been to clubs or anything like that." Except on raids, he thought quietly with a smile.

"Do you dance?"

"Sure, is that a hint?" His eyes sparkled and she almost retracted her question, but decided to let it stand. Why not?

"Well, this music is better than I thought—not the old 'my-truck-broke-down-and-my-girlfriend-left-me-for-my-best-friend' kind of thing. It has a beat."

"Sounds like a good idea to me." He smiled, standing as a new tune rocked the bar and more people crowded into the small joint. "Let's go"

She looked hesitant for a moment, but took his hand, letting him lead her to the dance floor. When they got there she seemed stiff and a little uncomfortable, but after a few minutes, she transformed before his eyes.

Moving like a sinuous wisp of smoke, her long, lithe body caught the beat of the music as her eyes closed and her arms raised above her head, the movements accentuating the line of her breasts and turning his mouth dry. He could hardly move for watching her.

Reaching out, he placed his hands on her trim waist, pulling her in a little closer, settling them into a rhythm together. She smiled and looked at him through heavy eyes, lowering her hands to his shoulders as the rocking music changed to something slower. Following his instincts, he gathered her in more closely, inhaling the scent of her. His body hardened, pressing intimately into hers, and he waited for her response, loosened his grip so she could move away.

She didn't.

"Want to get out of here?" he whispered close to her ear. The feeling of her moving against him was driving him out of his mind.

"What did you have in mind?" When her cheek grazed his as she drew back to look into his eyes, it actually made him shiver.

"A walk on the beach?"

She waited a beat, as if considering, and he held his breath until she answered.

"Sure. That sounds nice."

4

THEY WALKED slowly, hands clasped, not daring to speak lest the spell be broken. At least, that's how Logan felt, his blood slightly buzzing with alcohol, dancing and desire, his body burning to know what hers felt like, tasted like, inside and out.

How long had it been since he'd felt like this with a woman? Had he ever? Maybe once, a long time ago.

Inspired by Sarah, alcohol and a sense of freedom he hadn't enjoyed in a good long time, Logan felt for this one minute like he really was on vacation. It wasn't that his larger purpose for being here was fading, but there wasn't much he could do right now, and he was captivated by Sarah. They turned toward the beach and he set his concerns aside for a moment. Logan shut out everything but the light grip of her hand in his and the warm night air on his face. He didn't want to think about the things that he'd been obsessing over for months, only about the beautiful woman at his side.

They stepped up over a concrete beach wall, hopping down on the other side and landing in soft, cool sand. He thought he heard her laugh softly, and glanced over to see her head thrown back as she looked up at the stars, a whimsical smile on her face. She was the most gorgeous thing he'd ever laid eyes on, and his throat constricted.

"I wish I knew constellations. I can see shapes, but I don't know what they are. Or if I'm even seeing the right ones."

"Never took astronomy in school? I figured all kids learned the basics in science class."

She shook her head, a shadow crossing her features.

"I was home-schooled, then sent to a private school. My parents were against the standard scientific curriculum used in the public school system. As an adult, it's just not something I've pursued. Though maybe I will when I get back home."

"Ah." He paused, unsure how to respond. He didn't want to offend her religious beliefs, but he never understood why people couldn't be both devout and educated. His parents had had them all in church every Sunday, but it had never interfered with his broader education. They'd always encouraged him and his sister to know everything they could about the world, to have a thirsty mind.

After all, even the most religious people of ancient times knew how to use the stars for navigational purposes, if nothing else. Then again, Galileo had died while under permanent house arrest during the Inquisition after maintaining that the earth revolved around the sun, not the sun around the earth. Logan remained silent rather than voice his opinions—the night wasn't made for political arguments. But Sarah had already intuited his thoughts.

"It's okay. My family and I don't see eye to eye on…a lot of things anymore."

"So you don't share their religious beliefs?"

She shook her head, looking suddenly sad, and he didn't press. Not just yet.

"Well, I can point out some of the constellations for you, if you want to know."

Her face brightened again, and she smiled. It took his breath away.

"Please." She poked her finger up into the air, indicating a pattern she saw. "Is that something?"

"Yes. Here, see. You'll know this one." He pulled her over in front of him, snuggling her close and grasping her extended arm by the wrist, helping her make a connection from one star to another until she inhaled sharply.

"The Big Dipper?"

Logan smiled, loving the soft warmth of her up against him and the surprised pleasure in her voice. His head was clearing from the beer, but his blood was still buzzing.

"Right. I knew you would know that one. Everyone has to have heard of it, if not seen it."

"Show me another one."

He lifted her hand again, and drew her arm down, then across, in the shape of a cross.

"The Southern Cross?" she guessed hesitantly, and he dissented.

"The Southern Cross can't be seen from here. This

one is Cygnus, the Swan. But it is also known as the Northern Cross."

"It looks like a cross, not a swan."

He chuckled, inhaling the scent of her hair, the clean scent of her shampoo mixing headily with the ocean breeze.

"True. But see, the bird is in flight...this star is Deneb, Arabic for tail, as in the tail feathers of the bird. He's diving through the sky..."

She stared, silent, and he risked the moment to bend his face into her neck, losing himself in the softness he found there. Her voice hitched a little, though she didn't move away or discourage him.

"I guess I can see that."

Logan lost all interest in the sky as he turned her to face him and made it clear he didn't want to discuss stars any further as his lips found hers. They were alone on the beach, and it was dark all around them. Private.

There was no preliminary kissing, no get-to-know-you nibble, just hot, carnal plundering of each other's mouths, and he felt his knees shake and his body go rock-hard all over. She was softer than he'd imagined, and she moved against him in an invitation he wanted to accept, that his body insisted he accept. Unable to stop kissing her, he slid his hand up under her tank top, massaging her breasts through the thin cotton bra she wore, and swallowed her deep moan.

He moved his hands down, tugging her shorts lower and then pulling them down to her feet as he sank to his knees, running his hands over her, memorizing her shape and scent as he released her feet from her garments and nudged her thighs apart with kisses.

"More…let me in…"

She accommodated, though he sensed her hesitation, and he cupped her gently between her legs, investigating, reassuring. Her breath came quickly and she moved slightly against him. He looked up; her head had lolled to the side, her eyes closed, fists clenched. He smiled, dragging his tongue along the crease of hip and thigh where her skin had not been touched by the bug spray and felt her shudder, parting even farther for him.

She tasted like honey and salt, flowers and sex, and he groaned against her, wanting more. Widening her, he darted his tongue inward and was rewarded to feel her muscles jerk in a sharp response. He slid his tongue deeper, finding the sensitive nub of flesh he sought, a hot pearl hidden in between silky folds, and drew it between his lips, softly tugging.

"Oh…God…."

He pulled away just for a second. Her eyes were still closed, her face a study in mindless pleasure.

"Say my name, sweetheart, Sarah. Say my name when I make you come…."

His mouth was back on her, nibbling, nipping, sucking until her head spun, and she managed to whisper his name, wanting what he was giving her, needing it on a profound level that she could barely understand. She buried her hands in his hair and pulled him closer, focusing on the pleasure he was giving her as the shadows crowded around her.

She struggled. The usual demons danced around the edge of her pleasure-saturated brain, disappearing for a moment when she felt him slide one finger deep inside her, then two…. She could do it, she could enjoy him making love to her, set her thoughts aside and just feel what he was doing….

But her conscious mind reasserted itself and she opened her eyes, looked down… she tried to concentrate only on the pleasure as he knelt before her, but the deadening chill started in her chest, worked its way out as images flooded her brain, and what she saw invaded what she felt.

"Stop…Logan, ah, please…stop…."

He did, immediately, looking up in concern. He stood, his breath ragged, and she could feel the heat from his body emanating toward hers. This was so unfair. For both of them. She shouldn't have let this happen.

"Are you okay? Did I hurt you?" He reached to touch her, but stopped, unsure.

"No, no…" God, how could she explain this without seeming to be the worst kind of tease? She didn't want to tell him the truth, and grasped at some kind of rational explanation. "I just…couldn't."

She couldn't see his expression clearly enough to know what he was thinking, but she felt relief course though her when he backed off, bending to grab her clothes from the sand, shaking out her shorts and handing them to her. She slipped them on quickly, feeling awkward and miserable.

"I'm sorry, I—"

He tipped her chin toward him, and she made out a

smile. "No apologies, honey. This can only be good if it's good for both of us, and there's time."

Sarah sagged, feeling both relieved and saddened. He didn't understand that there might never be a good time for this. Not for her. Her mind was poisoned against it, even as her body pleaded for his touch.

He grabbed her hand and pulled her down on the sand beside him.

"C'mon, sit down."

"I'd better get going."

He paused, clearly unsure what to make of her response.

"Just sit for a moment."

She did, and he blew out a breath, looking out over the darkness of the Bay. "Can you tell me what happened?"

She searched for words, and didn't really find any.

"I just lost it, you know, it happens, maybe too much beer—"

Logan wasn't buying such a half-assed explanation, and it was his nature to talk about things plainly. "I'm not an expert, but I know enough to know you were close to coming, and something happened to pull you back. If not me, not something I did, then what?" His tone was rich with patience and warmth. She felt like an idiot. "You can tell me, Sarah. I wish you would, in fact. I don't like thinking I did something to chill you like that."

"Really, it wasn't you. Promise. I—I…it's nothing. Just a thing. I see a lot of…bad things, in my work. It gets to the point where I can't get them out of my head.

This isn't the first time it's interfered with me having a satisfying sex life, so believe me, it's not you." She looked away—it was all he was going to get from her. It was all she was prepared to give.

He was gazing at her too intently, and she needed to get away. She turned to get up, felt his hand on her shoulder.

"Listen, I'm sorry to push. You don't have to talk about it. I had a good time tonight. You want to get together and do something tomorrow?"

His request took her by surprise, and she blinked. Was he asking her on a date?

"Like what?"

"Something that doesn't involve alcohol, maybe?"

She smiled, feeling that little tug she always seemed to get with him. Surprisingly, she wanted to spend more time with him, even if it was going nowhere. Standing, she took a deep breath as he lifted up easily to stand beside her.

"Okay. I guess I could meet you at breakfast and we can decide then."

He stepped closer, and she felt her breath catch. He looked hot and handsome, and some of the tingle between her legs started up again, amazingly.

"And Sarah?"

"Huh?"

He leaned in, grazing her lips with a kiss that was light and yet incredibly scorching.

"You taste like heaven."

He took her hand and started walking back toward the inn without another word.

* * *

SARAH WOKE UP the next morning fully clothed and with the feeling she was terribly late. Late for what?

She glanced at her clock, struggling to clear her head. She'd slept late, exhausted after a restless night, to say the least.

Logan.

The events of the night before flooded back and she groaned. They had a date. How had she ended up agreeing to a date? Feeling heat invade her cheeks, she knew. Too many beers and too many nights alone had loosened her up just a little too much, softened her inhibitions. What he'd done had felt…good. Very good.

Abbreviated as it was, it was the best sex she'd had in a long time. Usually she didn't even get that far, but apparently the alcohol helped her move past some of her blocks. Just not enough. She made a face, recalling his surprise when she'd asked him to stop. And much to his credit, he had. Without anger or even a hint of impatience, with apparently no thought to his own satisfaction, he'd stopped.

If only he hadn't broken the spell when he spoke, maybe she could have blocked it out until she'd come. But that wouldn't have been fair to him, since she wouldn't have been able to go further.

What was she going to do now?

The inn provided breakfast between eight and ten, and it was nine-thirty. Her stomach growled, and she swung her legs over the side of the bed, stripping quickly and flying into the shower.

Regardless of her bad judgment the night before, she was hungry, and she didn't want to be rude. She'd said she'd meet him for breakfast, and she would. Now that her head was clear, she could get things back where they should be. He'd probably taken off by now, anyway.

LOGAN SAT with his cup of coffee, wondering if Sarah was bagging on him. He was beat, but looked forward to seeing her again in the bright light of day. He'd stayed up, his body raring to go, and he'd used the excess energy to work on getting that connection going again— with no luck. He couldn't work on it during the day when someone might notice; he had to do it at night.

And at this rate, he wouldn't be doing it at all. Looking out the window, he let the conversation around him fall to the background as he remembered what had happened the night before. He could still detect her slight scent on his skin.

It was almost ten. She hadn't come to breakfast, hadn't left a message. Something had sent her running last night, and she'd said it wasn't him—she'd been enjoying herself until something had gotten between them, and he wanted to find out what it was.

She said she saw bad things in her work, things that stuck in her head. Did she work with abused women? Children? In a hospital? Was she a rape or abuse counselor? Had she herself suffered such a violation? He'd had some training in that area, the basics all cops needed to know. It made him sick to think something like that happened to anyone, and it filled him with rage to think it might have happened to Sarah.

He took a deep breath. Or was she just snowing him, giving him some trumped-up excuse to put him off? Maybe he'd freaked her out going down on her like that? But no. She'd been into it, until something had chilled her. He wanted to find out what so he could chase those chills away.

He wanted to find out everything he could about Sarah Jessup. Tough as nails, he knew, she was also vulnerable and sexy—she kept herself protected, at a distance, and he wanted to break through. He wanted her again, as soon as he could make sure she felt the same way.

If he ever actually saw or spoke to her again, that is.

No sooner had that thought crossed his mind than he looked up to see her enter the room, sexy as hell in low-rider jeans and a cropped white T-shirt that sported the logo of a cheesecake store on it. The sight of her toned stomach nearly had him licking his lips. Instead, he focused on the sunglasses she was wearing even inside. She slid into a chair next to him, reaching for the carafe of coffee.

"Hungover?"

"Not quite, but definitely a little rough around the edges."

"Didn't sleep well?" He lowered his voice and let his tone suggest that maybe he was the reason why. It was clear by her grin she wasn't going to feed his ego.

"No, in fact, I slept like a baby…could hardly drag myself out of bed."

He peeked at his watch. "I can see that."

She looked at him over the top of her glasses in the way that he was starting to love and he saw her gorgeous eyes were only slightly blurry, with just a tiny bit of red that didn't matter at all. He wondered if he could get her to keep the glasses on in bed….

"Yeah, sorry about that. I tend to keep late hours, and sleep in the morning. At least, I used to, before—"

She stopped suddenly, and he was curious about the end of her sentence, watching her layer a generous spoonful of peanut butter over a flaky croissant—interesting choice. Sarah was nothing if not unconventional.

"Before what?"

She shrugged. "Nothing. Just work talk, and we decided none of that, remember?"

He watched her closely as she ate, mesmerized by the movements of her mouth, and curious about why she seemed almost relieved not to talk about work. His curiosity was going to have to wait for the moment.

"You're right. We did agree. A better topic is what we might do today."

Sarah stalled, watching him pop some grapes in his mouth as he waited for her to respond, not taking his eyes off of her. There was only one other couple left at the table, and they looked over at Sarah, still masked behind her dark sunglasses as she ate.

"There are museums littered all up and down the shore," the woman, a preppy twentysomething with a wholesome face and too much energy, said, waving her hands in enthusiasm. "We're doing a tour of them each day. Today we're going to the Debtor's Prison museum and the Railway museum. I'm a history major, getting my Ph.D. at Johns Hopkins, so I just can't get enough of museums. Dennis indulges me, though I know there are other things he'd rather do, but it's so hot out, and the museums are beautiful, especially these small, local ones."

She bubbled in her seat, leaning over to shake Logan's hand. "I'm Tansy, by the way. We're Tansy and Dennis DuBois."

Sarah had stopped eating midbite, wondering if she was going to have to administer CPR. The woman, who Sarah suspected might pass out before she got to the end of what she was saying, had barely taken a breath.

"That all sounds really interesting—" Logan was obviously trying to be polite. It didn't sound interesting at all as far as Sarah was concerned.

"Oh! I know!" Tansy popped around in her chair, grabbing the shoulder of an obviously adoring Dennis. "You could come with us! Are you here together?"

"No."

Sarah spoke the word a little more harshly than she meant to—she hadn't really meant to speak at all, but she wasn't taking any chances that Logan might agree that it was a good idea for them to go museum hopping.

"No you don't want to go, or no you aren't together?" Tansy seemed unfazed by Sarah's blunt answer.

"Both."

Tansy giggled. "Oh. You looked like you're together, and I overheard you talking about how you needed something to do. But, whatever, maybe we'll see you at dinner? Do you have plans for tonight? Dennis and I have no idea what we're going to do, but who knows?"

Sarah tried to smile, but her lips just wouldn't stretch that way yet. She needed more coffee. Logan picked up the ball.

"We just met here, though we're not here together, is what Sarah meant. Your invite is very kind, but I think we just want to wing it, and maybe we will see you later, but let's just see what happens."

Tansy twinkled at him happily. "Oh, that sounds perfect. If you two have just met you need time to get to know each other. You have a great day now!"

Dennis never uttered a word, not that he had had a chance, but he smiled before guiding Tansy from the room, his arm draped around her shoulders.

"Dodged that bullet." Sarah continued eating, relieved.

"They seemed very nice, if energetic," Logan offered diplomatically. "But I want you to myself today."

Sarah swallowed the rest of her croissant and reached for a handful of grapes, not so much hungry as forestalling the inevitable.

"I thought you might have taken off by now. You still want to do something?"

He seemed mildly surprised. "Of course. I wouldn't have ditched you. No way."

"It was rude of me to be late."

"Yes, so now you owe me."

She felt her back stiffen reflexively, and she took her glasses off, meeting his eyes directly. He was amazing-looking, and obviously a nice guy, but she wanted no confused expectations.

"No. I don't. I don't owe anybody anything."

A small crease formed between his eyes, and he put his hand up in a staying motion. "Hey, back down. I was just goofing around—I don't care that you were late. You're right, you don't owe me anything, and I'm sorry if that came off wrong. Let's just find something to do and have some fun, okay?"

Sarah sat back in her chair, feeling like a moron, but nodded. Fun didn't seem likely, but she was willing to try anything once.

5

SARAH PEERED DOWN at the blue water rolling gently under her boat, a seventeen-foot, bright yellow kayak. At first she'd had her doubts, but now that she was in the thing, it wasn't too bad. She could go forward and backward and, since she didn't intend to fall out, that was all she needed. For a city girl she was a decent swimmer. Though she hadn't spent much time in open water, she did laps at the pool several times a week. It was a habit she'd gotten into during her stint at the police academy.

The boat was, to her surprise, very steady in the water; even rocking it with her hips didn't tip it easily. She tested the kayak again, learning the boundaries as the instructor, Jim, had advised. Jim paddled easily among the people in the group, correcting and encouraging them. So this was the guy Ivy had the hots for.

He was cute enough. Though his granola-eating hippie looks weren't Sarah's style, he had a nicely toned body and a pretty face surrounded by shaggy blond hair. He was a flirt, too, and had smiled at her a little too much during introductions, until Logan had put the kibosh on that. Sarah watched Jim show a young brunette how to hold her paddle correctly; things weren't looking up for Ivy.

After she and Logan decided what to do, she'd simply donned a bathing suit top and shorts. Logan looked like a professional in his sexy, skintight black-and-green neoprene top and shorts. The suit fit so tightly that little was left to the imagination. If this was what men wore when they wanted to get a woman's attention, it was working.

Sarah had nearly stumbled when she'd met him downstairs before they'd left for their day on the water. She was glad most of him was hidden below the deck of the boat, or she would probably have missed most of the lesson. The attraction between them was hard to fight, but she was determined to try, since she knew it was bound to end in nothing but frustration.

As it was, the way the muscles in his arms flexed as he expertly guided his boat was distracting enough. She imitated his movements, trying to draw her boat around in a graceful arc through the water as he did so effortlessly. Normally she was very good at physical things, but this was taking some getting used to.

"No fair. You've done this before. How come you agreed to a lesson when you obviously know what you're doing?"

He grinned, and her heart foolishly skipped a beat.

"Well, you haven't done it before, and lessons are good refreshers for anyone. Besides, I don't know these particular waters, and it's always good to get some advice from someone who does." He nodded toward Jim. "Ocean waters can be tricky."

Sarah agreed, listening while trying to gauge the wind and the water, and how both were trying to thwart her novice attempts.

Logan spoke encouragingly. "Don't muscle it so much. You're trying to force the boat to go where you want with your arms. Don't use your arms, use your midsection, and keep your paddle more or less rotating in the same position. See? You don't have to force it."

He demonstrated, and she studied his movements carefully, then took a deep breath, doing as he said, and felt lighthearted—a feeling she wasn't particularly used to—when her boat swung gracefully to the left.

"Excellent!"

Nearly blushing under his praise and warm regard, she chastised herself silently, feeling like a goof. Concentrating, she practiced the move several more times, in several directions.

It really was kind of neat, she thought. Since she was living down here now, it was probably a good idea to learn to do more things on the water. Having had the resources of New York City at her disposal, she was often at a loss in Norfolk, a nice but much smaller city. Swinging her boat around, then paddling it backward and stopping, she smiled. Maybe she would buy one of these things.

"You're doing great. A natural."

It wasn't Logan who spoke to her this time, and she looked up to see Jim smiling at her in blatant admiration. Logan was oblivious, talking with an older man about something or other a few yards away. Sarah regarded Jim calmly.

"Thanks. It takes a little work, but I like it."

"You're picking the moves up more quickly than most. You're ready for the next step, learning to get in and out of the boat."

"I already did that."

He laughed, never letting his eyes drift from hers. "No, I mean you have to fall out of your boat, and then get back in."

"Why would I want to do that?"

"So if you fall out, you can get back in."

Sarah frowned. "I won't fall out."

But Jim was resolute, shaking his head. "Part of the lesson. You can't really go anywhere away from shore if you can't get back in your boat, or help your partner get back in his. Rules of the road, so to speak. C'mon, it'll be easy. I'll work through it with you."

Sarah looked toward Logan, who was still caught up in conversation, and sighed.

"Okay. What do I need to do?"

After a few times dumping out of the boat—though she still wondered who the heck threw themselves out of a boat that wasn't on fire on purpose—Sarah started to get her bearings. She felt like a drowned rat by the fourth time, but she could exit her boat and crawl back in, both with help and by herself.

As she hauled herself up and over for the last time, she was pretty sure Jim was checking out her butt—just as he'd slid his hand a little too far up her calf when he'd helped her in the time before. She'd had enough lessons for the moment and looked for Logan as she settled back in the cockpit of her boat, soaked and ready to do something else.

"So you've learned how to do wet exits."

Logan's boat slid quietly up beside hers, to her relief interrupting the space between Sarah and Jim. The instructor offered them a friendly salute and headed off to another member of the group.

Logan grabbed the lip of Sarah's kayak, butting them up against each other, side by side. She looked at him, shaking the wet out of her hair.

"A what?"

"Falling out of the boat upside-down on purpose. It's called a wet exit."

"Yeah, that's one thing you could call it."

He just laughed. "I know it seems stupid, but if you know enough ways in and out of your boat, and eventually how to roll it, you can take these craft in just about any kind of water, where no other boats could ever go."

"Fascinating."

"I thought you'd think so." He grinned. "We have the boats for the day, though the lesson's over. How about we go back and get some food and drinks, then we can go off on a paddle somewhere. Maybe Smith Island. I hear it's not a long trip."

"An island? Down here?"

"Just a small one off the tip of the shore, past the national wildlife refuge. We can travel back out from the beach, hug the shore and then it's about a fifteen-minute paddle across to the island. It's undeveloped for the most part, so we'll probably be alone."

The lazy suggestion in his words didn't fail to make her pulse race just a little faster, and in spite of her intentions to keep her distance, she agreed, and they went back toward shore.

THEY WERE PADDLING across an open stretch of water, their boats quietly cutting through the one-foot chop, and Sarah felt truly relaxed. Her muscles were loose and warm from the paddling, her mind at peace. Logan moved parallel to her a few yards away, but they said nothing. The early afternoon sun was hot, but she barely felt it in the breeze, and she smiled as brown pelicans swooped overhead, diving down headfirst into the water for their lunch.

They'd hugged the shore for the majority of the trip, paddling underneath a section of the incredible Chesapeake Bay Bridge and forward to the spot where they veered southeast toward a shore visible on the other side. Late at night Sarah had often watched the twinkling lights of the bridge from her apartment, and she'd driven over it several times, but paddling beneath it was yet another new perspective.

Considered one of the seven engineering wonders of the world, it spanned twenty miles above ground and included two tunnels underneath the Bay. The bridge connected the southern shores of mainland Virginia with the Eastern Shore.

Bobbing in the water in her small boat, she'd appreciated its enormity more than ever. She was enjoying so many marvels of man and nature on this short kayaking trip.

Sparing a glance over to Logan, who also appeared lost in his own musings, she thought maybe vacationing wasn't so bad after all. She saw him steer his kayak a little closer as they approached the island's shore.

"Okay, these waves are just going to pop us right up on shore, so just go with it, okay?"

She smiled. She felt young, like she hadn't felt in years. Riding the waves into shore was like riding an amusement park ride, and she laughed out loud with the joy of it. When she hopped out of her boat into the wet sand, she caught Logan's eye as he stood by his own boat. The ribbon of heat his gaze caused knocked her off balance, literally, and she felt herself fall backward into cool, deeper water.

Sputtering, she emerged, finding Logan directly before her, smiling.

"Losing your balance?"

"The sand is soft—this beach seems steeper than the other."

"It is." He sank down, accepting her lame excuse with a wicked, knowing grin. They played in the water, taking in their surroundings, until Sarah realized Logan had disappeared from her view. Water sloshed around her, and before she could call out, he popped up in front of her, splashing. She reared back, surprised, but his hands slid around her, yanking her up close to him.

"I wondered where you'd gone to."

"Checking for sharks."

"Right. I think you're the only shark in this water."

His grin seemed to confirm the fact as he planted a kiss on her mouth, then released her.

"I'm starving."

Sarah blinked, lifting her fingers to her mouth, and followed him out of the water. He continued to keep her off balance. It didn't feel too bad, really.

"Tell me, are there bugs everywhere around here?" She jumped, swatting at a fat, biting fly that made a strafing run at her head, and Logan laughed, digging down into his hatch and pulling out their small cooler as well as the familiar green can of bug spray.

"Fact of life. You have stuff washing up on shore, you have little stinging carnivores around, too. To them you're just another meal."

Sarah snorted, covering herself with the spray again. "So much for idyllic beach scenes."

Logan whipped out a large blanket and laid it over the sand, setting down the cooler. He put his hands on his hips. Dressed only in the neoprene shorts, he was darkening quickly, his chest and limbs turning a light tan.

"I don't know, Sarah. I think this is pretty idyllic, myself. Perfect, really."

Her name on his lips caught her breath; she liked it. And, bugs and all, he was right. She looked out over the water, listened to the quiet around them. It was beautiful here. She threw him the spray can.

"True. I can't believe all the shells—there are so many of them, and they're big, not like the little scraps I find on the mainland beaches."

"No one bothers them here. The birds and the bugs take what they want, and the rest is left alone."

She squatted to check out a particularly large oyster shell. Oysters were one of the creatures that had once filled the Bay, she knew from a little local research. There had been so many oysters they'd formed large reefs that were a danger to boats. They'd also provided food for native peoples over the ages as well as filtering all the water of the Chesapeake each day. No small task.

The small, fleshy creatures with shells so lumpy and ugly on the outside but so pretty on the inside were struggling now, endangered, just like everything else that lived in these waters. Sarah ran her fingers along the smooth, pearly inside of the shell, and a well of hope and sadness rose within her. This was a big shell. Maybe there were more? Or was it the last?

She set it back down on the sand, straightening to discover Logan's eyes fixed on her. Feeling oddly exposed, she walked briskly over to the blanket and plopped down, crossing her legs and reaching for the cooler.

"What did Harold and Karen pack up for us?"

He didn't say anything, but cleared his throat, sitting down beside her, maybe a bit closer than she was comfortable with.

"Not sure. Let's see."

They pulled out thick sandwiches wrapped in white paper and plastic to protect the food from the ice in the cooler, and found small plastic containers of salads, fruit and cheeses. Several kinds of nonalcoholic drinks lay flat on the bottom of the cooler and were icy cold in Sarah's hand as she pulled them out, sending a shiver down her arm in spite of the sun and heat.

"This is great. I haven't been on a picnic like this since I was a kid."

"Yeah, I can't say it's something I've done recently, either."

"No family events or romantic dates in the park?"

Logan bit into his sandwich, assessing her openly as he chewed and swallowed. "Fishing, Sarah?"

"Just making conversation."

"This is the first romantic picnic I've been on in a long time. Years, in fact."

She didn't want to admit how nice that made her feel, and just ate her salad because she wasn't quite sure what to say. Logan was making it clear he was interested in more than just buddying around, and she didn't know if it could be more than that. The fact that she wanted more, though she found it hard to admit, shook her, and the next words out of her mouth emerged from her anxiety as much as anything else.

"So is all this just a way to get in my pants again?"

The words cut through the air harshly, and she felt more than saw him draw back, his surprise at her response clear. Well, too bad. But instead of relenting, she dug in. She was too used to squaring off, and in her experience, that's what it was all about with guys. Why put pretty dressing on it? She took a deep breath, ready for confrontation.

But then he laughed, which was not what she'd expected.

"You do just lay it out there on the table, don't you?"

She shrugged, feeling her ire deflate in the face of his good humor, and bit into her sandwich. "Why sugarcoat things?"

He popped a ripe strawberry into his mouth and seemed to be considering her response.

"Well…we're attracted to each other, that was obvious last night. And I think you know I'd like to see that—more—happen again."

He ate another strawberry, slowly, his eyes on her with uncomfortable intensity. "But I also like your company. I'd like to think there's more to this—and to me—than just trying to get in your pants, though that thought is a very nice one, I have to say."

Well, at least he was honest; she'd give him that. And she was attracted to him, tempted in ways she'd thought were over and done for her. He was…unexpected.

"I'm not sure it will work out that way. Just to let you know, since we're being up front."

"You mean because things didn't go well last night?"

She nodded, not saying anything more, and almost jumped when he took her hand, running a half-bitten strawberry along her palm and then lifting it to his mouth. She inhaled sharply as his tongue lapped the sweetness off the sensitive part of her hand.

"So you don't like it when I touch you? When I do something like this?"

"I, uh—" Sarah lost any sense of what she was about to say when he took her index finger and slid it between his lips, and then drew it slowly out. His mouth was hot, and she made the mistake of looking down and meeting his gaze, then letting her eyes travel down a little farther where he unabashedly displayed an erection that challenged the tensile qualities of the neoprene.

She looked around, not so much concerned whether they were alone as making sure they were. If she'd been worried about his motives, she wouldn't have come. Even if she was wrong, she was more than up to the task of taking him down if things got out of hand. But, as he continued to lick hot kisses all over her fingers, and that gorgeous erection still strained within clear view, taking him down was not the first thing on her mind. Well, not in the violent sense, anyway.

She closed her eyes, trying to shut out the thousand sparks of desire he was igniting. She didn't want to feel these things.

But then again, why not? It was a vacation thing, right? In two weeks he'd head home, and so would she, and that would be the end of it. Maybe this was her chance to reclaim a little part of her life. Maybe it was time. No harm, no foul.

Remembering what he'd done to her the previous evening, she was surprised at how tempted she was. She was rarely seriously tempted by men, at least not so long as she could remember. But she was burning now.

"Sarah, you never answered my question. If you don't like this, all you have to do is tell me to stop. Just like last night. If you ask me to stop, at any point, I stop. No problem."

He slanted a mischievous smile, glancing down at his

crotch, where her eyes had been planted just seconds before. "Well, maybe there's a bit of a problem, but not
one you have to worry about. I mean it."

If he'd pressured her at all, she could have withstood
the temptation, written him off as just another guy trying to find a way to get laid.

As it was, she just pushed her dishes aside and
twisted, closing her hand over his forearm and lifting
herself, snagging his leg and ending up solidly on top
of him, pushing him into the sand as she lowered her
lips to his. She pressed herself along her entire length
while she kissed the breath from him, leaving him in no
doubt about her intentions.

If she was going to do this, she was going to do it
her way.

She felt a rumble in his chest, a laugh, maybe, or a
groan, maybe both, as his hands closed over her buttocks and pulled her against him while they continued
to kiss, forgetting about the need to breathe. Lifting up
for just a moment, she saw him smile, his voice both
husky with desire and teasing.

"Smooth move. Someone took some self-defense
classes at the local Y?"

She just smiled, opening her legs and locking her
knees around his hips, pushing back against him before
leading another assault on his mouth. Classes at the Y.
Yeah, right. If he only knew.

And then somehow, before she could take her next
breath, she found herself flipped over on her back.
Logan planted himself heavily on top of her and settled

between her sprawled legs, his hands pinning hers on either side of her head. She smiled up at him, a little kick of admiration filtering through her.

"Pretty smooth, yourself. You must have had those same classes."

"Yeah, something like that."

She waited, watching him stare down at her, apprehension and anxiety starting to brew as she wondered what he was planning. Why didn't he just do it already? Kiss her or something? Hadn't she made it clear she was willing? And ready, she thought, feeling his hardness pressing between her legs. Lord, was she ever ready. She was hot all over, and it wasn't from the midday sun.

But if he waited much longer she might lose her resolve, and she would have to back down, again. She fought the thoughts crowding her mind. She didn't want that to happen.

"Logan—" Her voice held an edge of panic and he freed one hand, and brought his to her face, gently wiping away some sand and pushing her hair back.

"Shhhh, Sarah. Relax. We don't have to make this a contest of wills. We can both win."

"But—"

"Shush." The command was gently issued, barely a whisper, but it worked. She didn't usually take well to being bossed, but these were…unusual circumstances.

He leaned down and rubbed his mouth over hers, releasing her other hand and framing her face with both of his. Something told him that he needed to show her more than desire, something more than sex.

It surprised him that this woman, for whom he had no intentions beyond sex, could inspire such tenderness inside him. He wanted to make her feel…more. More than good. More than hot.

Beautiful as she was, she had a toughness about her. She was too prickly, too ready to fight. It intrigued him, since many of the women he'd known romantically had been too accommodating for his tastes, too eager to please. But Sarah made him curious; he wanted to find the soft parts, the ones she had hidden. He slid his hands into the short, spiky silk of her hair. Yes, he wanted to know everything soft about her, inside and out.

"You're perfect," he whispered huskily, caressing the curve of her face with his eyes before burying his face in her neck, leaving hot kisses all along her neck and shoulder until she was arching into him, baring her skin to him.

He pushed his groin into the warm V between her strong legs, delighting in the fierce need that made him want to rip his shorts off and get inside her now, and the equal desire to take it slow and have her begging for him. She was a strong woman and that made it all the more necessary for him to know she was as desperate as he was.

Sliding back, he sat up on his knees, looking down at her flushed cheeks and passion-smudged eyes, drawing her up into a sitting position. He lifted her top, pulling it over her head and exposing her to his eyes, the sun and the ocean breezes that brushed her nipples, stiffening them even as he lowered his mouth to the tempting buds.

She was nicely proportioned, firm, muscular, but sweet. As he drew at the hardened pebbles in the middle of all her softness, he listened to her breath quicken, felt the shudder work its way along her form.

"Logan, please…"

"Yes…beg me to touch you so I know you need me as much as I need you."

She tensed for a moment, and he knew what he was asking, knew she probably never begged for anything, but he wanted to hear her beg for him. When he pushed her breasts together and suckled at them both the pleasure was so excruciating pleas tumbled from her lips as she grasped the back of his neck and pulled him in tighter, urged him to suck harder. He was happy to accommodate, happy to give her whatever she wanted, though he took it slow, savoring every taste, every scent as he worked his way down her body, trying to discover her secrets.

With an impatient curse, she maneuvered herself forward, dragged her hands along the planes of his back and found the edge of the flexible fabric of his shorts. She slid her fingers underneath, working it down.

"Sarah, wait…"

"No, no waiting." Her need was heroic and reflected in her voice as she wriggled against him, working to get them both naked.

"I don't have any protection. I wasn't planning on…"

She scrambled to her feet, thumbs hooked at the waist of her shorts, looking down at him, and he thought he'd never seen a woman more magnificent. The sun was high, casting out its brilliance behind her, and she looked like a warrior. This wasn't a woman who would beg—not for long, anyway. She spoke, shucking the shorts and standing before him gloriously nude.

"I'm protected. Unless you have something you need to worry about, it's been a long time for me. A very long time. I'm clean. And I'm ready."

He blinked, then grinned. "Okay, then. No problems here."

He pushed his shorts down off his legs and flung them to the side, turning over to lie back on his elbows, unashamed of letting her see how turned-on he was. He barely had time to brace himself when she fell to the ground, tackling him again. He laughed into her kisses. So much for begging—this was a woman who was fully prepared to take what she wanted. Thank God she wanted him.

"How long?" he managed to sputter as she lifted over him, easing him inside of her with a look on her face that nearly did him in. She was so damned tight and wet he almost lost it in a way he hadn't in years. But as she settled down, encompassing him, he held on.

"What?" she was breathless, already starting to rock on top of him, her fingers digging into his shoulders. Before he could repeat his question, he felt her tightening around him, her voice ragged, her breathing sharp. "Logan, I'm sorry, this is going to be quick…."

Hardly wanting apologies for her amazing hunger, he watched her let go, moving as she needed to, coming fiercely around him, squeezing him tight inside and with her thighs, crying out in release. The milking action of her muscles nearly drove him over the edge, too, but he managed to lie back, keeping his own pleasure at bay, at least for the moment.

Apparently it had been a *very* long time for her, and he was in no hurry. He wanted this to last. He wanted to feel more than the basic physical connection with her that he was feeling at the moment, but he opened himself to her, letting her do as she liked, his own body straining in response. There'd be time for more later.

"Again, Sarah. Take what you need."

She looked down, leaning over him so that her face was close to his, her mouth closing over his. The next time she came, moving over him with such intensity that she took him with her, they were both moaning inside of a hot kiss as the world fell away around them.

Holding on to each other in the aftermath of their intense joining, something stirred deep inside him: undeniable physical satisfaction mingling with a sense of unease, a feeling of something left adrift, disconnected. What had happened between them had been sheerly physical, and he wasn't complaining, but he knew he hadn't reached her past the surface. And for some insane reason, he wanted to.

6

"So, HAVE YOU been behaving yourself?"

Sarah rolled her eyes, thinking about her recent behavior, and of how surprised E.J. would be to know she was taking a page from his book and living in the moment. Love the one you're with, or some such thing. But she was in the middle of the main room of the inn; it wasn't the time or the place to share. So instead she kept to the real reason she'd called in the first place.

"Please, E.J., help me out here."

"No way am I inviting the wrath of Ian down on my head, darlin'. He's been a knot of nerves since he found out about Sage, and if he finds out you aren't enjoying yourself as ordered, we'll both be used for target practice."

Sarah sighed heavily into the phone before a smile reluctantly twitched. Ian had just found out Sage was pregnant and according to E.J., he was freaking out. She could easily imagine it. But really, she was so happy for Ian and Sage, and for herself, in an odd way. She'd been estranged from her own family for so long, been alone for most of her adult life, that it was weird—but nice—to be part of a group again. They felt like her family.

"So she's doing well?"

"Healthy as a horse, and not giving Ian an inch, though he's trying to boss her every which way. He wants her to put a hold on her work for now, and you can only imagine her response to that. Fur is a-flyin'. And I think he wants to drag her into some kind of shot-gun wedding, to boot. I saw them this morning and she looked healthy enough—she was chewing him out one but good. Hormones, maybe—she was really on a tear."

Sarah laughed. Sage was no pushover, though she wasn't usually argumentative. There was no need to be—she and Ian worked together like peas in a pod, and it almost made Sarah think romance might be worth the trouble. Ian was usually putty in Sage's hands, but they were both strong personalities, and every now and then, as E.J. described, the fur certainly did fly.

"Good luck to him. Sage will never give up work, he's got to know that. She's fought too long and hard to get where she is. As for the wedding, well…that ought to be interesting."

"True, but it won't keep him from trying. I think he'll settle down as things move along. He just needs to know she's okay. On some level he's just scared to death."

Sarah knew Ian's first wife had miscarried and had al-most died from the complications. Ian, an FBI agent at the time, had been away on a job, and it had been the be-ginning of the end for their marriage. She could imagine the conflicting emotions her boss must be going through at the moment, but she knew he could handle it.

"It's good for him."

"I agree. So how about you? Enjoying your time off in the sun and sand?"

"It's dull, though I've found a few things to do." She closed her eyes, picturing Logan on the sand as she'd ridden him the day before, finding pleasure that had rocked her soul. They hadn't seen each other since they'd returned. They'd had dinner, talked about nothing in particular, and shared one hot kiss before retiring to their separate rooms. He'd seemed distracted, and she wasn't going to nag or push. He was probably just tired.

But Sarah had to admit to being disappointed that they hadn't spent the night together. He'd opened a Pandora's box; now that her body had been reintroduced to sex, she wanted more while it was available.

But he hadn't been at breakfast that morning, and no way was Sarah going to go all girly and start waiting for him to show up. They'd had a good time, but she had a life of her own.

"I just thought you could mail me over those reports. I could get a little reading done, you know, while I'm sitting on the beach."

"Are you getting a tan?"

"I wear sunblock, so no."

"Good girl, but if you don't come back looking a little sunkissed and completely refreshed, Ian is likely to send you on permanent vacation. He'll want evidence of fun. So no, no work. No reports. They'll be waiting for you when you get here."

"Can't you just tell me what they say then—"

"Have fun, Sarah—bye."

And he hung up, laughing, the devil. She growled, setting the phone back in the cradle with a frustrated bang, forgetting she was standing in the middle of the main room where her bad temper was on display for anyone passing by. Damn the lack of privacy here!

She stood by the base of the stairs, fuming. She refused to give into the impulse to find Logan, though there was a nasty little voice in the back of her brain that taunted her. *He got what he wanted, why should he bother looking for you now?* She felt her eyes burn as she closed them with effort. She would not fall back into that trap again.

"Are you okay?"

Opening her eyes when she felt a hand on her elbow, she found Ivy staring at her with concern. The young woman spoke gently to her again.

"Come here, sit down. Did you get some bad news?"

Sarah shook her head, sighing, letting Ivy pull her to the plump sofa in the corner.

"No, just a frustrating call."

"You looked liked you didn't feel good."

"I have a headache." Sarah knew she sounded bitchy, and she didn't really have a headache, she just wanted to be left alone. Looking into Ivy's open, honest face, she immediately felt bad.

"You stay here, let me get you something. Some aspirin."

Sarah reached out, grabbed her arm as she started to rise, and attempted a smile. "No, really, thanks. It's not that bad and I don't take pills of any kind."

"Ever? Not even vitamins or aspirins?"

"Nope. None. Ever."

Ivy looked at a loss, and Sarah felt like an ogre for always putting the young woman on the defensive when she was just trying to be nice. She made an attempt herself, changing the subject.

"I'm sorry. I just need to sit for a while. But thank you. How are you doing?"

Ivy seemed taken by surprise at the apology and the inquiry, her brow creasing before she smiled, her eyes lighting up.

"Oh! I do have news! I have a date." She said the word proudly, beaming.

"With the kayak instructor? Jim?"

Ivy nodded enthusiastically. "I bumped into him last night, in the office, and we got talking, and then, boom, he just asked me out. I was such an idiot, I couldn't say anything for like five minutes, but he was so nice. He didn't seem to mind how dumb I acted."

"You're not dumb. And you're not an idiot. Don't talk that way."

"Oh, I know, in general. I'm smart enough for college, and smarter than a lot of folks. But I always get so tongue-tied around guys, and especially around him. He's just so… I get shivery whenever I look at him."

Her voice had gone all dreamy, and Sarah felt a surge of uneasiness, a reminder of days when she, like Ivy, had been unsuspecting of what men were capable of.

"Are you sure you should go out with him, Ivy?

Alone? Maybe you should make it a group date until you know him better."

Ivy's eyes shadowed, and the furrow in her brow returned. "Why, I'm sure he's very trustworthy—he's been working at the resort for several years, and Karen says she trusts him implicitly."

Hmmm. Shows how much Karen knows, Sarah thought sourly as she remembered Jim's flirting the day before. She was sure the guy had only one thing in mind when he looked at Ivy, fresh, innocent and ripe for the picking: easy target.

"Listen, Ivy... I don't want to burst your bubble, I really don't, but be careful around Jim. Have some fun, but don't let him charm you into anything you don't want to do."

"Like having sex, you mean?"

Sarah was surprised at the girl's candor, and relieved—maybe Ivy wasn't as naive as she'd thought. As naive as she had once been.

"Yeah, for one."

Ivy's cheeks stained with a light pink, and she leaned in toward Sarah. "I haven't done that with anyone yet. Not all the way, anyhow. But isn't it better to have a guy who's older for your first time? Maybe he knows more, you know, what to do?"

"Could be. But I met Jim and I just have a feeling you should be careful."

Ivy drew back. "Really? Why?"

"He just seems kind of...you know, like a guy who gets around. He flirts, a little too much."

She smiled. "You mean in his lessons. He's always like that. It's just part of how he puts people at ease."

Sarah fought the urge to roll her eyes. She hadn't felt at ease when Jim was sliding his hand up her calf the day before. The guy was a shark.

"Ivy, older guys know things, true, but take it from me, older women know a few things, too. I'm just saying, be careful with him. Don't let him use you."

Ivy's eyes clouded over, and Sarah stood, putting her hand on her shoulder. "I know you have a crush on him but believe me, he's not as trustworthy as you think."

Ivy looked up, a few sparks in her eyes now. "How can you know? You don't even know him!"

Sarah sighed. "I've known plenty of guys like him. Believe me, the more you keep your distance, the better."

With that, she smiled thinly and walked toward the stairs. The talk with Ivy about men using women had fired up her ire toward Logan. She would go about her day, but not before she had a few words with him first.

LOGAN OPENED one bleary eye, looking up and seeing only the ceiling. God, he was still dressed and still on the floor, where he'd finally spent hours working once he'd broken back into the wireless connection. He didn't even remember falling asleep, though it couldn't have been all that long ago. His laptop had fallen into sleep mode as well, the screen dark, a small, bouncing basketball the only indication the machine was on at all. He had to pack everything up before it was discovered by housekeeping, but first he needed to clean up.

He stood slowly, cursing the fact that at thirty-four, he'd left the flexibility and stamina of his twenties long behind. His back protested painfully as he walked toward the bathroom. Shower. Hot water. Food.

Sarah.

The basic needs occurred to him one by one, the last one making him frown as he stripped and stepped into the spray. He'd wanted to bring her to bed with him last night, pull her through the door and repeat what they'd done on the beach—and more—until he couldn't walk for other, better reasons. But he wasn't here for a fling. Sarah was great, and he wanted to spend more time with her, but it was going to be a daytime affair—his nights were spoken for.

And he'd made some good progress. He'd definitely tracked the names of two of the missing women to the gaming company's master list—now he just had to find out which boat they'd been on. Melanie had been missing for almost six months, but these other two had only been missing for two.

There were only two ships that made port at Norfolk and Virginia Beach. He'd spent the better part of the night trying to break into the company computers, but it was far beyond his capabilities to get through their security. He'd been banging his head against a brick wall for hours before he'd finally lost his connection and had fallen asleep while trying to get it back.

But the evidence was mounting, and he knew the next step was trying to get on board the ship. However, doing that would be tricky. He had no jurisdiction here, let alone out there where none of the laws applied. That was a snag he hadn't quite counted on. But if he could get out there, get some solid evidence, and bring it back—

A loud knock on the door startled him out of his train of thought, and he hurried out of the bathroom. His laptop and the papers lying all over the floor had to be hidden away.

"Just a minute!" He let the towel drop, scrambling to shove everything under the bed. He would put it away properly once he got rid of whoever was knocking.

Wrapping the towel securely back around his waist, he opened the door, surprised to find Sarah—looking a bit riled—on the other side. Her blue eyes flashed, first with anger, then with something else as she let her gaze drift over him. His body responded with a quickening that was almost embarrassing.

"Sarah."

"Logan. You just got up?"

He ran a hand through his hair, feeling awkward and half-aroused. He glanced back at the bed to make sure nothing of what he'd kicked underneath showed from where he stood.

"Yeah, I'm sorry—were we meeting?"

"No. We weren't. Forget it, sorry to bother you."

Her voice was cold and she started to turn away when it hit his sluggish mind that she thought he was giving her the brush-off. He'd parted ways with her last night—when it was clear she wouldn't have said no to spending the night together. And then he'd failed to show up this morning. Now he was acting like he barely remembered her. He couldn't blame her for being pissed. He sighed, holding his hand out to her and opening the door a little wider.

"I'm sorry, sweetheart. I'm just groggy." When she didn't reach for his hand he moved forward, catching the door with his heel, standing close to her. "I was up late, couldn't sleep and then overslept this morning. I thought it was housekeeping at the door, and just didn't expect to find you there."

She seemed to bristle at that, stepping back. "Fine. I'll leave you alone, then."

He snagged her hand. "C'mon, come in. It'll take me a second to throw some shorts on, and we can go get some food."

"Already ate."

He tugged her hand, pulling her up close against him. "I'm sorry I was a dumbass. I missed you last night…."

"You didn't have to." The meaning of her words was obvious, and he felt his response catch in his throat when she spoke again, her features softening just a little. He felt like a jerk for hurting her, and swore to make it up, starting right now. "What were you doing that kept you up so late anyhow?"

"I tossed and turned for a bit, then got caught up in a book."

"You were reading all night?" She was outright skeptical now.

"Yeah. I thought about coming down and knocking on your door, but I didn't know if you would appreciate being awakened at that hour."

"It must have been some book. Maybe I should borrow it."

"I'll give it to you when I'm done."

Her voice softened, "Well, I guess I shouldn't have my nose so out of joint. I was late to meet you yesterday, after all."

He smiled, remembering yesterday. "Let's just not worry about any of that, huh? We're on vacation, right? Off the clock?"

They stood silently for a moment, and her eyes drifted over his bare chest, the towel he'd almost forgotten he was wearing. She must have forgiven him; color pinched her cheeks. Without a word he pulled her toward him and closed the door, pushing her up against it, and kissed her before she could say one more word.

The kiss should have left her with no doubt about the fact that he'd missed her, but even as he searched her mouth, ran his hands over her curves, he felt a sting of guilt for lying to her. He pushed it back. The two things, what he did with Sarah during the day and the case he worked on at night, had to be kept separate. He didn't want *anyone* knowing what he was up to.

When her hands yanked impatiently at the towel, leaving him naked and pressed up against her, he smiled, enjoying how forthright she was about her wants and needs. It was daytime now—Sarah time. He intended to enjoy it and leave the night behind, for now.

"I think you're overdressed." His voice dropped an octave and he saw her lips open slightly as she took a deeper breath, and then smiled. She'd forgiven him.

She ran her hands over his chest, stopping to tweak his nipples in a way that brought his cock immediately to attention. He didn't feel sluggish now, that was for sure. He pushed the spaghetti string sundress she wore up her waist and past her gorgeous breasts and kissed every inch of skin as he revealed it. The pink lace bra she wore hinted at a sweetness, a femininity, that provided contrast to her tough demeanor. It totally turned him on and he groaned, sucking a dark nipple through the lace and pulling gently with his teeth as it budded in between his lips.

She buried her hands in his hair, directing him, but this time he intended to stay in charge and shook her hands off, exploring the swell of cleavage at his own pace, working her panties lower as he did so. Soon, they were both naked.

Leaning down, he snuck one arm under her knees and the other behind her, slipping her away from the door and up into his arms as he carried her over to the bed. The look on her face was one he'd carry with him forever—open desire and sheer surprise—apparently, Sarah had never been swept off her feet before.

She certainly hadn't. Sarah was too surprised to protest when Logan swept her feet from under her, though she felt silly and touched all at once by the gesture, enjoying the feel of his hard arms holding her, but smiling as she watched her feet, still wearing her sandals, flopping around out in midair. Being so tall, she'd never really thought of herself as portable, but Logan made her feel like a feather. It was nice. It seemed like everything he did was nice.

Any anger she'd had about his absence that morning died a swift death as he laid her down and covered her from head to toe with his body, warming her and touching her everywhere. She couldn't think straight, he was everywhere, and when he nudged his thigh between hers, pressing up where she was melting for him, she groaned and arched into him, rubbing against him harder.

Sarah couldn't believe she was ready so fast, on the edge and urging him to do something—anything—to push her over. She wanted it hard and fast, like before, but, maddeningly, he took his time. She raised her head to object, but he shushed her.

When she shifted up onto her elbows her body moved just enough so that his chin was in line with the shadowy spot between her thighs. He smiled in a way that had her heart racing, and her objections caught in her throat.

When he pushed his face between her legs, nudging until she opened for him, she fell back to the pillows again. His tongue circled her clit, hot and slick, and she nearly lifted off the bed when her orgasm hit her. Panting, she opened wider, inviting him in for more.

He peered up at her, his eyes clouded with desire. Watching him lave her, his tongue darting out and tasting her, she felt a tide of affection and desire—no ugly thoughts or images assaulted her—and something that had been locked up tightly inside of her finally broke free.

Then he moved, and she felt his fingers probe, sliding inside, exploring her depths until she was blind to anything but everything he was making her feel. Just as she hovered on the edge again, he stopped, pulling himself up and covering her.

They looked into each other's eyes, and Sarah swallowed at the tenderness she saw in his. Her scent surrounded them, and she rose to kiss him experimentally, finding that anything seemed to taste good on those lips of his, even her own essence. She deepened the kiss, partially because she loved kissing him, but also because she was a little afraid of how deeply he was looking at her, and what he might see when she was open to him like this.

But he wasn't going to let her be afraid. Pulling back, he reached down, sliding one hand beneath her hip, and held her steady as he thrust inside her, deep and hard, and stayed planted there, rotating his hips in a delicious grind against her, never letting her eyes leave his.

"Tell me a secret, Sarah." He pressed deeper, and she moaned, hardly able to hold a conversation. But he kissed her, refusing to pull out but maintaining the torturous pressure of staying deep inside her, until her gaze met his.

"Why?"

"I want to know something about you. While I'm this deep inside you, I want to know something about you that no one else knows."

Sarah tried to wiggle, tried to move, to ease the need and the unbearable fullness, but he weighed her down, held her firm. Why did he want this from her? Wasn't what she was giving him enough?

Her breathing was uneven, her mind blurred with pleasure and the increasingly urgent desire for release as he placed one hand between them, rolling her nipple almost casually, causing her to shudder.

"Just…one…secret…Sarah." He kissed her face, punctuating his words. "Just one small thing about you that no other man knows."

She bit her lip, searching his face. "Then I want one from you."

"Deal."

He pulled all the way out of her and she gasped with the wonderful friction of it, confused—she hadn't told him a secret—but then he thrust back in, deeper, harder. She dragged her hands down his back, squeezed his ass, pulled him against her and felt him tense. Two could play.

"Okay. Um, I've never had food sex."

He blinked, then smiled. "Not even with whipped cream?"

She shook her head, pressing up against him, sighing when he moved just a little.

"What kind of food sex do you fantasize about?"

"You want details now?"

He slid from her body in one long, leisurely pull, and then plunged back into her, making her cry out.

"Yes."

She was aching for relief, but she managed to gasp out her one small food fantasy. She'd read about it in a book once, and had never been able to forget—and had never had anyone to share it with.

"Peaches. You have ripe, juicy peaches…you slice them open. You rub them all over each other, Lick the juice off…oh…"

He smiled, kissing her ear, swirling his tongue inside it in such a way that she lost all coherent thought for several seconds. She'd never known her ears were so sensitive.

"You rub them everywhere? Even here?" He licked lightly behind her ear, down the curve of her neck to her shoulder, and pumped into her slowly.

"Yes, there…"

He lifted up, moving down her body, his mouth everywhere, on her breasts, the indent of her waist…

"Here?"

"Yes…yes…. Oh…"

He was kneeling back now, hoisting her up by the hips, holding her firmly as he increased his pace, urging her to come, reaching down to press with his finger along the wildly sensitive flesh of her sex as he asked, one final time, "Here?"

"Yes!" Sarah screamed the word as the pleasure finally released and raged through her, throbbing through her limbs and out to her fingertips, nothing existing but Logan, who was still thrusting in a quick, steady rhythm. Gathering herself as much as she could, wanting to see him lose control, she saw his jaw set, knew he was close.

"You…tell me, Logan. What are your secrets?" She reached up, scoring her nails over him lightly, watching his eyes flash, then blur, with pleasure.

Leaning down over her he whispered his hot wishes

in her ear as he groaned out a release that sounded as powerful as hers had been. She listened closely to his secrets, none of which could be done at the moment— but they had a lot of time ahead of them, and not much else to do. As he collapsed over her she smiled, looking forward to keeping busy.

7

SARAH ROLLED OVER, disoriented and tangled in sheets, but she didn't get far before a strong, warm arm hauled her back against a very manly body. Logan.

She could hardly believe it; they'd slept right through lunch. She rarely slept like this, let alone with someone. She looked at the clock; it read half past one.

"I'm starving." Logan growled against her shoulder, pressing against her, and she laughed, falling back.

"You can't be serious. Again?"

It was his turn to chuckle. "I meant literally starving. For food. I never had breakfast, remember? You stalked in here and seduced me, and now I'm faint from hunger and exertion."

She wound her arm down under the covers, wrapping her fingers around his erection.

"Yeah, I can see you're about to pass out. And for the record, you seduced me."

"I meant the second time."

"Oh. Yeah, that was my fault."

"I might have a little energy left, but then I'll really need food."

She took pity on him, rolling over to kiss him, offering a final, promising squeeze and then sliding out of bed, extending her hand to him.

"C'mon. Shower, then a late lunch."

"But…." He looked shamelessly down at his jutting cock and then smiled at her.

She walked toward the shower, sending him a sly look. "Maybe we can take care of that in the shower."

He raised his eyebrows, looking interested. "You think so?"

She just smiled and disappeared behind the door, hearing his footsteps seconds behind her.

"Line or net?"

"Net. There's no way I'm touching that stuff."

Logan took the plastic container of chicken necks and salted eel. "It won't bite you, but the crabs might."

"I'll risk it. That stuff stinks."

"Just chicken and fish parts. Don't be such a girl."

She stuck her tongue out, testing the weight of the long-handled net in her hands. The inn was having a bring-your-own crab dinner. They had arranged local licenses, rented equipment and given everyone maps and instructions. Whatever you brought back, they'd cook and provide the side dishes. Sarah had her doubts, but Logan seemed to think it would be fun. So here they stood on a dock, Logan attaching a slimy piece of bait to a hand line while she waited with her net.

"We aren't going to have to eat them whole, are we?"

"You don't like softshells?" He sounded shocked. She wrinkled her face, thinking of the time she'd gone out to dinner with Ian, E.J. and Sage, all raving about soft-shell crab like it was the nirvana of food. Far from it, in her opinion.

"They look like fried spiders. I hate the way the legs hang out over the edges of the bun."

"That's the best part! You can bite them off before eating the rest."

She shuddered, wondering if they'd let her order a hamburger for dinner. Logan dropped the line into the murky wetland water.

"Don't worry, I'm sure they can come up with something else. Probably crab cakes."

"Now you're talking. I love those."

"This is the place for them—of course, Maryland is really the crab cake capital of the world, but I won't be too picky about state lines."

"Should we really be eating these? Aren't they overfished?"

Logan nodded. "It's a problem. The entire center of the Bay is protected water—no one can take blue crab out of water deeper than thirty-five feet, since the spawning crabs travelling from the north end of the Bay need to be protected. Some people think there needs to be more protection on the rivers and places like this, but there's also the financial draw, the support for places like the inn and local restaurants." He looked out over the Bay. "It's a balance between protecting the crabs and making a living. We won't take anywhere near as many as the license allows us to. If we manage to find any. Might be burgers tonight after all."

He winked at her, and she forgot about the crabs and wondered how long this would take. She wanted to get him back to the room. But before her thoughts could wander any further, he yelled in delight, lifting his line carefully.

"I guess my fears were unfounded. Let's see what we have here."

He pulled the line up very slowly, making sure not to dislodge the creature hanging from the end. Sarah brought the net down underneath as soon as she could reach, capturing the small, wriggling creature.

"It's so small."

Logan fished it out of the net. Avoiding the small claws, he turned it over and inspected it. Sarah watched it move, entranced by the pretty, soft blue shell. He held it up so she could see better.

"Meet *Callinectes sapidus,* the blue crab. The Latin translates to 'savory beautiful swimmer.' This one is probably too small. She'd make a decent sandwich maybe, but the law says she gets put back to go grow up and make more little crabs someday."

Sarah frowned, looking closely. "How do you know it's a girl crab?"

"See this triangular section? It's called the apron— indicates we have a female. When she's mature, it will be rounder, bluer, more defined, with a little point at the top. She's got a ways to go yet."

Sarah watched him toss the crab back into the water.

"So you've done this a lot? You know a lot about crabs."

He nodded. "My parents took us out all the time when we were kids."

"You have siblings?"

Sadness permeated his features, and she stayed silent. The mood had shifted in that moment, and she'd apparently stumbled onto something painful for him. Rebaiting the line and dropping it back into the water, his voice was low.

"I had a sister."

Past tense. Sarah put a hand on his shoulder. She respected pain, and privacy.

"You don't have to get into it."

He was quiet for another few minutes, turning his face to kiss her hand lightly. "It was a long time ago. Her name was Mary. She drove me crazy."

"Younger?"

"Yeah. I was thirteen, she was ten, and it was her mission in life to drive me out of my mind."

"I imagine you did the same to her."

He smiled slightly, remembering. "Yeah. We excelled at aggravating each other." He sat back, sighing, waiting for another pull on the line, but none came. "She and my mother were killed in a car accident. Drunk driver. They died at the scene. My dad was a state cop, and by some cruel twist of fate he was the first car to arrive at the accident."

"Jesus."

"Yeah. I've stopped wondering what she would

have grown up to look like, how life would have been different if none of it had happened. There's no point, I suppose, in wondering. That doesn't stop you, though."

Sarah lined up behind him, warming him with a hug from behind, unsure what to say. There weren't words to deal with that kind of hurt, that kind of loss. He wrapped his hands up around hers.

"Dad lost it after that. The guy who killed them did a year and was back on the road. Dad started drinking, lost his job. Before I hit college, he passed on, too. I think he just gave up."

Sarah felt a chill run down the length of her body. Logan had essentially been left alone at thirteen. Lost everyone who meant anything to him before he was even close to being an adult.

"You lived through it. You survived."

"It's a blur. I don't remember the years after Mom and Mary died too closely. I tried to help him, tried to—" He cut himself off, shaking the memories off like water. "It was hard, but I got through. There were some family members who came around, who tried to help, but there was only so much anyone could do."

Sarah sat, honored that he'd told her but unsure what to say. They'd been physically close, but this brought them to an entirely new level. And she didn't know how comfortable she was with that. This was supposed to be a fling, but with just a few words, Logan had taken them somewhere she wasn't sure she wanted to be.

Not that she had a choice, it seemed. She squeezed him in her arms, feeling for the grief he must have suffered, and understanding some of it, though in a different way. She supposed in cases like this it was normal to share something back, but she wasn't going to do that. She couldn't. Another tug on the line saved her from having to worry about it as he turned his attention back to the line, and pulled it up again.

"Get the net—this is a good one, I can feel it."

She picked up the net, at the ready, glad to have the solemn mood broken. She looked down—he was indeed pulling up the largest, bluest crab she'd ever seen. She reached down with the net, securing it, and pulled it up on the dock. Logan put his hand on her arm, cautioning.

"Be careful with the big ones—those claws can grab hold and not let go."

Raising her eyebrows, she took a step back. The large crab had a lot of spunk, facing off and clicking his claws like mad. He didn't care that he was a lot smaller—he had more arms, and he was ready to use them. Sarah smiled, respecting the crustacean's attitude.

"Hey, tough guy."

"Uh-oh." Logan's voice interrupted her, sounding ominous.

"What?"

He sighed. "I know that sound, that tone of voice. You won't want to make crab cakes out of him, will you? You like him. You think he's cute."

Sarah blew him off, making a loud raspberry at the crab.

"Nope, he looks like dinner to me." She looked up.

"Will we need more? He's pretty huge. And you know it's a he?" She was still confounded by how someone could tell the sex of a crab, but hey, Logan did seem to know his biology.

"Yeah. So you don't want to throw him back?"

She shook her head resolutely. "No, since he's a he, we can definitely cook him."

"Ouch. I say that for all mankind, crustaceans included."

She grinned. "Sorry. But I do like crab cakes, and I won't feel too bad if we're only taking this one."

"That's the spirit." Logan put on a pair of heavy gloves and approached the crab from behind, picking him up carefully and tossing him into a deep pail.

"Let's head back."

THEIRS WAS the biggest crab, though others taking part in the picnic had caught more than they could eat, so there was plenty of crab for everyone, and many funny stories to go around. Sarah polished off her third crab cake, and turned to catch Logan watching her, an odd light in his eyes. A warmth that created an answering heat in her. She spooned up the last bite of crab and dipped it in mustard sauce, offering it to him.

"You think you can lure me with that bait?"

"I stand a fair chance. It's not everyone I would let have the last bite."

"I must be special."

The words floated between them, and she decided to neither confirm nor deny.

It was dark outside; the backyard of the inn had been transformed into a fairyland lit with Chinese lanterns, flowers and trees budding everywhere around them, the spicy aroma of crab and other assorted foods in the air. Everyone laughed, talked and ate—including Sarah and Logan—until it neared ten, and she felt him start to pull away.

Deciding to face the issue head-on, she looked him in the eye and called a spade a spade. "Are you a vampire or something?"

He looked at her blankly, obviously confused. "What?"

"Well, you always start to tense up when it gets late, you become distracted, distant…the party is just getting started here, and the night is young, but I can feel you pulling yourself away." She took a deep breath, not losing eye contact, forcing herself to say the words. "Are you married, Logan?"

"No! For Christ's sake, no, I'm not married. What kind of guy do you think I am?"

He seemed truly shocked and offended, but she wasn't going to let it throw her.

"Fine, that's good. So what is it then?"

His look became guarded, and she knew she had him—she just didn't know what she had him on. A different approach was called for. Somehow she knew he wouldn't be pressured or nagged into telling her what he was up to, and she really wasn't one for nagging anyway.

She leaned in, running her hand over the muscles of

his forearm, finding her way into the crook of his neck where she planted a few wet kisses, feeling the pulse at the base of his throat beat more strongly. Whispering in his ear, she reminded him of the things he'd said to her on the beach—his secrets, his fantasies—and asked him to spend the night with her so she could make a few of them come true.

How was a guy supposed to resist an offer like that? Logan felt his entire body go up in flames at her whispered suggestions, and went rock-hard when her hand drifted from his arm to his thigh. He had work to do, he had arrangements to make—he needed to get on board that boat, to find out what had happened to Mel—so why was he finding it almost impossible to think about his work with Sarah's scent surrounding him? Suddenly he didn't seem to want anything but her touch, and to be inside her, sleeping next to her….

His mind reared back, protesting—he'd just met this woman, and he was letting her distract him from a goal he'd spent months pursuing. He was letting his little head lead the way, and that wasn't like him. He owed Mel—she'd been his friend, and he had to stay on track so he could clear her reputation. Maybe even find her, though his gut told him that wasn't going to happen. If Mel was alive, she would have contacted him if she could; he believed that.

But even thinking about the case couldn't dampen his response to Sarah's seduction. He tried to ignore the way her tongue darted out and tasted his skin—he was going to have a hell of a time getting up from this table—but he had to try to concentrate on what was important. He liked Sarah, but he had to keep things controlled, mostly himself.

"I—I, uh, I'm just a little tired. Remember I didn't sleep much last night, and it's been a um, busy day."

She laughed huskily by his cheek, not about to give up. "We slept into the afternoon. I'm wide-awake." She drew back, leveling him a seductive look that nearly knocked him off his seat. "And I want you. I want to spend the night with you."

Then she added the one word that really killed him, knowing her as he did. Her eyes locked to his, she simply said, "Please."

Sarah realized both things were true—she did want him, and she did want to spend the night with him, more so than she had imagined—but she also wanted to see if she could break through this mystery of why he always dumped her at the doorstep like a princess about to turn into a pumpkin. She didn't even mind doing a little light pleading—it didn't feel wrong. In fact, she knew it would touch him. And from the look on his face, it had.

She wanted to know that whatever it was he did at night, he was willing to give it up for her. Or she wanted to know what it was.

He was hiding something, obviously. She looked around, glad to see that they were more or less alone, the other couples milling about near the food at the center of the garden. She slid her hand up his thigh, pressing against the erection that was hard to miss. She was obviously having an effect on him and that pleased her.

"Let's go back to the room. Yours, mine, I don't care. I don't want to be alone tonight."

He groaned into her neck, straining against her, and sighed his resignation. "Yours." The word emerged as a groan as he found her mouth in a hot kiss, and she responded victoriously. Whatever he'd been doing with his nights, it couldn't be all that important.

They stood and made their way around the edge of the garden and to the back stairs that led up to the second floor, to her room. Sarah's heart beat like mad as she pushed the door open, pulling him in behind her quickly and stifling the urge to giggle. She hadn't brought a man back to her room in at least seven years. She hadn't had the urge to giggle for longer than that.

The giggle turned into a laugh as she danced backward, feeling turned-on and powerful, giddy with the prospect of the night before them, the fact that he had come back with her, had chosen her over anything else.

He stood still, looming and masculine, watching her in the dimly lit room, seeming out of place in the more femininely decorated space. She crooked her finger.

"I want to help you make a few fantasies come true tonight, Mr. Sullivan."

She heard his sharply drawn breath as he stepped forward. "Do you now?"

She unbuttoned the blouse she was wearing, sliding it slowly from her shoulders.

"But since we're on my turf, I'm the boss. You just do as you're told." Her tone was playful but demanding— she held her stance as he stood still by the side of the bed.

"What if I don't agree to those terms?"

She shimmied out of the short skirt, standing before him in a matching black thong and bra. "Then I guess I'll just have to convince you to see things my way."

The sounds of the party still going on down in the garden lifted up through the screens, and she shivered as she felt the cool breeze waft through the window. It felt like rain was in the air; an early-summer storm was brewing. Maybe that was responsible for the electricity she was feeling.

"And how are you going to do that?"

She stepped closer. "I have my methods."

He stood with his hands by his sides and she stopped directly in front of him, just a breath away from touching him.

"You have too many clothes on." She reached out, sliding her hands underneath the summer-weight sweater he wore, pushing it up and over his head. He didn't resist, not that she'd expected him to. Leaning forward, she lowered her mouth to drag her tongue over one of his flat, brown nipples. Looking down she saw he'd bunched his hands into fists, but didn't move otherwise. She drew back and smiled at him, touching the thin, white scar on his shoulder.

"What happened?"

He looked down, as if he'd forgotten the mark was even there. "Got in a fight when I was a teenager. Rough times, short temper. The other kid had a knife."

She leaned in, licking along the scar, murmuring sweet nothings.

"You taste good."

"Anything to please."

"Really? Anything?"

His eyes, seeming almost black in the low light of the room, fixed on hers and he nodded. She stepped back.

"Take the rest off for me."

He slanted a smile, releasing his belt and unzipping his khakis, removing them in slow, strong, masculine movements. She took a deep breath, signaling to him to continue, and he did, removing his briefs and socks until he stood there naked and completely aroused, waiting for her next command.

"Do you trust me?"

He nodded and looked much more confident than she felt. She'd never done anything like this before, never had this much control, with the responsibility of trust placed firmly on her shoulders. She'd never realized how delicate it was, to hold someone else's fantasy in your hands, to make it come true. It meant something to her that he was willing to trust her, and she was going to make sure he didn't regret it.

"Come here."

He did, and she pulled a padded wooden chair from where it stood by the wall, and indicated to him to sit. He did.

"Put your hands down by the sides."

He hesitated just for a second, then did as she said, and she left him for a moment, rifling through one of her drawers, and pulled out two pairs of hose. Efficiently, quietly, she bound his hands and ankles to the chair. When she rose to stand in front of him, she thought she detected a slight apprehension in his gaze, and the unexpected feeling a rush of power and arousal stunned her.

"Are you comfortable?"

"Not entirely."

"What hurts?"

He looked down at his lap, his erection straining toward her, assuring her he was more aroused than ever, and that it wasn't the bindings that bothered him.

Reassured, she walked in a circle around him, watching him and smiling wickedly. "So, where should I start? Here?" She fell forward, bracing her hands on each of his shoulders and taking his mouth in a smoldering kiss, leaving him panting and straining harder by the time she drew back, strategically brushing the tip of his cock with her thigh. "Or here?" She let her mouth dip to his chest, kissing him in as many tender spots as she could find leaving little nips along the way until she had the satisfaction of feeling him pull against the bindings.

"Here, maybe?" She settled down on her knees, grazing her fingers over his sac. His head fell back on a loud gasp, his chest heaving with excitement.

"Oh, I know. *Here*...." She moved forward, her own heart slamming in her chest as she did something she'd only done once before, and silently prayed she did it well enough. Spotting the drop of dew at the tip of his penis, she touched it with her tongue, tasting the salty sweetness of him, and found herself compelled to taste more. She wanted to know all of him. Moving closer, she took him in her mouth, glorying in his strangled groan, the tension of his bound limbs, and suckled gently before sliding the rest of the way down.

"Oh, Sarah…"

She moaned against him, the vibration eliciting another shudder from him before she really lost herself in exploring him this way, the taste and scent of him fueling her desire as she encompassed him over and over, touching him everywhere she could reach and becoming frustrated with the bonds herself, wanting access to all of him.

Standing up, her chest heaving, a slight sheen of perspiration covering her skin, she practically ripped off the thong and bra, approached him like a cat, draped one long leg over the side of the chair and straddled him. As she was kissing him she reached down, positioning him, and enveloped him inside her in one searing thrust. Her hands wove into his hair as she continued to kiss him, holding him captive as she clenched him tightly inside. He broke away, his words ragged against her skin.

"Sarah…ah, I need to touch you…please."

His gaze landed hungrily on her breasts, and she stared back at him, shaking her head in the negative, denying his request. She cupped her breasts, pinching and rolling her stiffened nipples, arching back, taking him deeper and sighing his name as she moved faster, pleasuring herself and letting him do nothing but watch and feel.

Their sounds filled the room, panted promises and

murmured pleas, the slap of flesh against flesh until neither one could hold out and their cries of release rose up together, merging with the sound of fat raindrops hitting the windows and the laughter of partygoers running inside from the sudden shower.

Sarah continued to rock against him, wrapping her arms around his shoulders, burying her face in his neck, catching her breath. After a few moments she slid from his body, silently untying the silk bonds. His hands slipped under her arms, drawing her up and pulling her into his arms to experience the most tender kiss she'd ever known.

IT DIDN'T HIT her until deep into the night that she was alone. They'd made love through the storm, falling into an exhausted sleep wrapped around each other. The absence of the heat of his body woke her from a disturbing, restless dream, and Sarah sat up in bed.

"Logan?" She spoke into the empty room, and there was no response. A chill worked its way down her spine as rain still slapped against the windows, sparkling droplets clinging to the glass as she slid from the bed, felt around her closet for a robe and put it on.

He wasn't in the bathroom; he was gone. A cold feeling settled in where only warmth had been before. She found her slippers and left the room. The door to his room was shut, but she turned the knob a little and it pushed open. Nothing was ever locked around here. Stepping inside, she found only darkness.

"Logan?" Her whisper carried through the empty

room again, with no response. She wrapped her arms around herself, stepped in a little farther and reached for the light on the bed stand. Where could he have gone?

The bed was made; he hadn't been here. She swallowed a sense of dread; the room suddenly felt empty to her, as if its occupant was long gone. Had he left? Why would he? Looking for a sign of his presence, she opened a drawer, finding socks, pants and underwear, and then spotted several fat manila envelopes under the clothes. And a laptop.

A laptop? Here? She looked closer. It wasn't anything fancy, but how weird to have it here. Did he know about their policy before he came?

Picking up one of the envelopes, she hesitated. She shouldn't be doing this, no matter what. Even if what they had wasn't just a fling—and she was beginning to wonder if that was all it was—it gave her no right to paw around in his personal things.

She leaned down to replace the envelope, gasping when the flap fell open and a sheaf of papers—photographs—fell out.

As she looked down and bent to gather them, her stomach churned. She saw the photos of women scattered on the floor. Pornographic pictures of women in compromising positions, hardcore shots that smacked of a professional job. A small cry escaped her lips.

They were Logan's. He was involved with pornography? It didn't seem right, but, as her aching heart reminded her, shame washing over her while she stared at the photographs, it never seemed right. It was always the guy next door, the one you would have suspected last. The one who'd just made love to you.

So this is what he did at night? What he was hiding from her? He was holed up in his room with a laptop and a porn collection? Was he collecting or just browsing? Buying or distributing? Professional or amateur? She made herself look again—it wasn't anything she hadn't seen before—and noticed many of the pictures were of one woman. Was he stalking someone? Was she a favorite?

She clutched the robe around herself, suddenly feeling dirty and shamed. She hadn't let herself feel like this for a long time, and her mind raged at the return of the familiar sensations of being used, humiliated.

Her heart hardened over the ache. She'd find out, damn him.

"Sarah, what—"

She twisted around and found him standing in the doorway, his expression unreadable as he saw she'd discovered his secret. She stood, too, letting the rest of the papers and photographs fall from her hands to the floor, facing him. What now? She was alone, without any resources whatsoever except her own wits. No one knew except the two of them. She was on her own.

He stepped into the room and closed the door and she took a deep breath, steadying herself. He sounded normal when he finally spoke.

"I'd just gone downstairs to get something to drink. When I came back up, you weren't in bed. I saw that my light was on." He shook his head, running a hand through his beautiful sable hair. "Shit, Sarah, this is really not a good thing."

She almost laughed, too many emotions coursing through her to name as she fought to keep control of the situation. She would keep control—her life might depend on it. She schooled her features and calmed her voice, staring him down.

"You've got that straight, slick."

8

THEY STARED each other down for several seconds and he took in the tension in her muscles—she was poised for a fight, not just guilty at being caught going through his things. Did she think he was some kind of pervert? He blinked, realizing that was exactly what she was thinking.

"Listen, Sarah, I'm not going to hurt you. I'm not— those aren't mine."

She swiped him with a look of disbelief that would have had a lesser man cowering, and he took a heavy breath before speaking again.

"I mean, yes, they are mine, but it's not what you think. They're not personal photos, they're for work. My work. My job."

That sent her eyebrows up, and had her eyes flaring even more furiously than before. She held her rigid stance. "Yeah, I can tell. It's obviously professional work. Are you the photographer or the distributor? No— wait." She stemmed his immediate objection. "There'll be time to get into that later. But you need to tell me one thing, and if you lie to me, I can promise you, you're going to regret it big time."

He took the bait. "What's that?"

The rest of the color drained from her gorgeous face, though her eyes remained cool as slate. "Did you take pictures of us? Have you taken any hidden shots of me while I didn't know, because if you did, or if you lie to me about it—"

"Sarah!" His voice bellowed in the small room, cutting her off. Whatever he'd expected to hear her say, it wasn't *that.* How could she think he was even capable of such a thing?

"There's no way I would do that. Not to you, not to anyone. I told you, if you will give me a damn second to explain, this is all a part of my work." He stepped forward, putting his hand up to stop the next biting comment she was ready to spit in his direction.

"I'm a cop."

They both backed up a pace. He knew he'd spoken, but he could swear she'd said exactly the same words, at exactly the same time.

"You're a cop?"

Again, in perfect unison that echoed between them, they asked each other the same question. As they started to speak again, Sarah held her hand up this time.

"No, stop. Okay." She paused for the moment. "You go."

He nodded. "I'm a cop in Baltimore. A detective. I'm looking into a case, those women in the pictures have come up missing. I'm trying to find out what happened to them." He held her gaze. "You're a cop? Did I actually hear that, or am I going crazy?"

It hit him for the first time that maybe his department had taken his defection seriously. Had she been sent to watch him? But then why would she be so surprised and mistakenly assume he was a pornographer? She couldn't think he had anything to do with Mel's disappearance, even the thought of that made his blood boil, and he was wrenched from his thoughts by her staccato response.

"Norfolk, Virginia, Computer Crime Unit."

"Wait. You're not here to check up on me?"

"Why would I be?"

He didn't reply right away, unsure now of how much to tell her. This was an unexpected development, to say the least.

"So you had no idea who I was before we met?"

She looked down pointedly at the stack of photos in his hand. "I'm not sure I have any idea who you are right now. But no, and I repeat, why would I?"

He took another step into the room, aware that she was still guarded—an understatement, she was ready and apparently willing to kick his ass, if need be—and crossed to the bed.

"Relax, Sarah. Let me explain."

Famous last words, her eyes seemed to accuse him, but she reluctantly closed the gap between them, pulling a chair up and sitting by the corner of the bed, a safe distance away. Her suspicion hurt, but he tried to get past that and consider how she must be feeling. It was probably a shock for her, to say the least, to discover that the man she'd taken as a lover had a stash of porn in his dresser drawer. And if she was who she said she was, it was even worse. She thought he manufactured the garbage.

She threw the stack of photos to the bed, and they slid into an array of images sprawled over the bedspread, ending where he sat. Regarding him with hard eyes, she crossed her arms and legs. He almost smiled. In her robe she looked sexy and tough, making him want to delve into her soft places yet again. But it was clear that wasn't going to happen, at least not at the moment.

"So, slick, go ahead. Explain."

"I wish you'd stop calling me that. And you said you were from Brooklyn. How is it that you end up being a cop from Norfolk?"

She just continued to stare at him, so he gave in. "Okay. Me first. See this woman?" He picked up one of the more debasing pictures and showed it to Sarah, trying to sound objective, debriefing her on the case like he would any other cop.

"Her name is Melanie Vincent. Detective Melanie Vincent." He stopped again, looking at the picture and seeing past the ugliness of it into Mel's sweet face, her strong face, the mouth that had often smiled at him, and swallowed hard. "She was my partner almost five years. We made detective at about the same time, worked together every day, and a lot of nights."

Sarah remained silent, but he felt the weight of her gaze upon him. He looked away from the picture, setting it back on the bed, and filled Sarah in on the rest of the story. Mel's troubles, the suspicions about her questionable behavior, her disappearance, the pictures, and what he saw as the betrayal of the department that had given up on finding her.

"Sounds like she had some serious problems. She's alive enough in those pictures—why do you think she did anything but go AWOL and find a new career for herself?"

He felt every muscle in his body tighten in rage. "Do you have partners? A person or people you work with closely?"

She nodded.

"Do you know them? Really know them, trust them and feel confident when they've got your back?"

"Of course." She thought of Ian and E.J., who were closer to her than some of her own family.

"So would you be so willing to write them off if something similar happened?"

He had her there, he could see the understanding flicker in her eyes, but only for a second.

"Okay. So you're working on this solo? Why would they send you in alone?"

"It's a little more complicated than that."

"What's that supposed to mean?" Leaning forward, she narrowed her gaze, focusing on him like a laser. He thought she must be hell in an interrogation—but she'd said she was a computer cop, did they do interrogations? He'd only known feds in that field.

"Logan, in what capacity, exactly, are you working on this investigation?"

"I'm on my own—not exactly with the support of my department."

She didn't react, not overtly, but he saw the flicker in her eyes and she sat back.

"They don't know you're working on it?"

He shifted on the edge of the bed, his lips flattening in displeasure at having to explain. But in for a penny...

"This vacation was kind of an informal suspension. They wanted me to get my head together, forget about Mel, and I have one more chance to go back to my job. I was told if I touched the case again, so much as spoke about it, I was fired."

Sarah blew out a breath, obviously comprehending the spot he was in, and he didn't know if he should be thankful for that or not. At least she seemed to believe him, but would she turn him in?

"You were lovers? You and Detective Vincent?"

"No."

He couldn't tell if she believed him or not from her steady glance, but it was true. He and Melanie had never had anything romantic between them. It was all about the job. And the friendship.

"I want to make sure you're who you say you are. And from what you're telling me, I can't exactly call your department to double-check."

"I have my shield, but you know anyone can pick one of those things up on online auctions—you're going to have to either trust me or turn me in."

He hoped desperately that she opted for the former.

"You're right. Okay, so how about you tell me about your investigation, what you have so far. Maybe I can help."

"Uh," he grunted, not quite sure what to say. Help? He hadn't expected that. And he wasn't sure he wanted her involved. This was his personal business. Letting her into this was like letting her into one of the deepest parts of his life, and, well, she was the woman he was sleeping with. He looked at her now, with fresh eyes, and yeah, he could see the cop, but he didn't want to.

He cared for her. He hadn't thought about that too deeply, but he knew she was more than a vacation fling. He liked her, but enough to let her help him with his case? A strange sense of apprehension and protectiveness overcame him as he struggled for a response and found none. She saved him the effort.

"I saw the laptop—do you have records I could look at? How have you been…?" Awareness dawned on her features. "You're the one that's been hacking the inn's connection!"

"How'd you know that?"

She slanted a smug grin in his direction. "I shut you down, babe. It was smart of you to hook in at night when you thought it would go unnoticed, but you didn't count on the fact that Harry works on his books at night. He noticed his connection had slowed down, and had me look at it. I closed you out."

He put two and two together quickly, realizing she had been the source of his frustration that night. Now it was his turn to ask some questions.

"How long have you been on the force? What exactly is it you do? Were you a fed?"

She put her hands up to stem the flow. "Hey, whoa.

You're the one going rogue here, so stop with the third degree. I really am just here on vacation."

"You want in on my investigation, you answer some questions." He could be stubborn, too, and he wasn't just going to let her have the upper hand that easily.

"You're pretty cocky for a guy one phone call away from being fired."

"That won't stop me from working on the case, it would just make things a little harder." He shrugged, hoping she didn't call his bluff but refusing to take a subordinate position to her threats. "You want to make that call, you call."

She regarded him with grudging respect. "Fair enough. No, I wasn't a fed. I was a hacker."

"A criminal?"

"Hell, no. I won't say I never broke the law, but I functioned more as an informant to the feds, helping them get underground information on Internet pornography operations." She smiled when she saw his surprise. "That's right, you're messing around in my playground, babe."

"So when did you join the force?"

"A little over a year ago. They were putting together a special unit, a high-level computer crime operation, an experimental thing. And they recruited me based on my work as an informant."

"You're a rookie? Jesus…" He slapped a hand to his head, looking shocked.

She was up and standing before him, looming and mad as hell. Gorgeous as hell. Sexy as all get out. "I am *not* a rookie. There's no such thing as a rookie in our unit. I went through accelerated academy training, and I've never been a street cop, true, but we've brought down more sleaze in a year than most operations do in five. And I have more computer expertise than you can imagine—obviously, since I was able to shut you down."

"So you're a cop behind a desk, working on a computer?"

"No. Do you think we can arrest people by computer? That we do it over e-mail? Jeez, slick, don't be stupid." She pulled her robe to the side, exposing a length of perfect thigh, and indicated the bandage. "Not a biking accident like I told you. Sorry. I was chasing a perp and fell on some glass. Believe me, I can hold my own when I need to."

"I'm sure you can, but there's no way I'm letting you in on something this dangerous, Sarah."

When her eyes flashed with fresh temper, he took a chance and reached out, grabbed her hand and pulled her down beside him. She didn't resist his touch, which he took as an encouraging sign.

"Listen, as far as I know these women could be dead. There haven't been any new pictures on the Web site for a while—there's no evidence of it being more than a one- or two-time deal with each one. So what happened to them after the pictures were taken?"

"Maybe they were sent elsewhere? Sold? Put out on the streets in a foreign country?"

His stomach clenched at the thought. "Mel would

have found a way out. Regardless of her problems, she wasn't that kind of person. If she could have gotten out, she would have."

"So you think she's dead." Sarah's voice softened slightly and she squeezed his hand. "I'm so sorry for that, Logan. But since you're all alone in this, you need me even more. If you are trying to track them down on-line, believe me, I can help you more than you can imagine. I have resources that—"

"No, I'm done with the computer searches. I'm taking it to their doorstep now."

"And where would that be?"

He wasn't about to tell her and she knew it, her full lips thinning.

"Listen, I can find out whatever you know, and faster than you did, believe me—you told me her name, and that's all I need. So I'm in on this—deal with it, or deal with your captain."

"You're blackmailing me?"

"Such an ugly word, but if that's how we have to play it, so be it. You are on your own, and you're looking at some pretty ugly crimes happening in my backyard."

Every muscle in his body tensed in response to her aggressive response, and he almost jumped back when she leaned in, slid her arms around his neck and pressed herself up against him. Was it only a few hours ago that they were lovers, and he was buried inside her, all of his secrets tightly kept? Where did this leave them? What were they now? Still lovers? Partners?

He didn't like it, but he slid his hands around to her

back, unable to resist the softness of her body next to his. Confusion jammed his thoughts. These were dangerous people he was dealing with. He wasn't about to let Sarah end up as one of their victims, even indirectly.

"Just let me help, Logan."

"Why? You're on vacation, why would you want to get caught up in this mess?"

He pulled back, looked down into her face, softer now. She had feelings for him, too, he knew, though they'd have to sort all that out later. Maybe it was just sex, but maybe not. There wasn't time to figure it out now. Still, it didn't stop his body from reacting to the closeness of hers, her warmth, her scent.... He saw her blue eyes melt as she put her hands on his shoulders.

"I couldn't care less about vacation. I hate being on vacation, and I would have found a way to go home the second day if I hadn't found you." The blurted confession made her suddenly uneasy, and her eyes shifted from his to the pictures on the bed. "This is my job. I want to help you. I want to help them. It's what I do. And I'm good at it—believe me."

He didn't say anything, just soaked up her earnestness and her beauty, emphasized by her real passion for her work. He would bet she was excellent at her job, but that didn't mean he was going to take advantage. This was his fight, Melanie was his friend.

And Sarah was...well, she was not the right person to be working on this with him, for a lot of reasons. The fact the he was hard for her right this minute, sitting here beside her, struggling because all he wanted to do was push her back and slip inside her, was among the chief reasons working together was not a stellar idea.

"I don't think we should work together, Sarah. It's just not a good idea."

"I told you, it's not really your choice. I can help you wrap this up quickly. Let me in, tell me what you know. What you have planned."

He hesitated, knowing that his next words were going to come between them like a large, cold wall, but that was how it had to be for now.

"No. I can't do that. I don't want you involved in this."

"Too bad."

Now she was just pissing him off, on top of arousing the hell out of him.

"This is my fight, Sarah. My case. My friend, my research, my time into it. My risk with my job. It's nothing to do with you."

She didn't respond, but he could see her chest expanding and contracting more quickly beneath the sheer robe—he'd gotten her goat, too. He expected her to go head-to-head, and he braced himself, but then she surprised him, her voice so soft he had to strain to hear.

"There's another reason I do this. Another reason I want to help. It's important to me, in a very personal way."

"How could it be? You didn't know them."

She turned away, walking away from him to look out the window that offered a view of the quiet street below.

He didn't follow, but just waited for her to speak, unsure what to expect.

"Because I've been there. Where those women are. Used, exposed. Humiliated. Just like that."

She couldn't have shocked him more, and he did stand, jumping to his feet, and then hesitated, unsure whether he should hold her or leave her be, too many responses flying into his head for him to articulate one before she continued. He stood his ground, listening.

"I was in college, in love, everything was perfect. I'd had a hard time convincing my family to let me go to a regular school—they wanted me in a faith-based college or a women's school, but I wanted to study computer science, and MIT was the best offer I had."

"You were at MIT?" He was impressed, not that he felt his Penn State education was anything to sneeze at. But MIT was, well, MIT.

She nodded, taking a deep breath, her face impassive.

"For two years. Top of my class, proving to everyone, including my family, that I could make it on my own, excel in my field." She wrapped her arms tightly around herself. "Then I met Guy, and everything seemed even more perfect. A total computer god, handsome, funny and apparently nuts about me."

"I find that easy to believe."

She smiled, but just a little. "Yeah, I did, too. Too easy. I thought we were in love, so I slept with him."

"Your first?"

She nodded. "He was wonderful, taught me…a lot. We did things that I wasn't always comfortable with, but

I figured when you loved someone…well, you tried to make them happy. And I enjoyed it, mostly."

She shook her head ruefully. "My mother found birth control pills in my medicine cabinet when my parents came for the weekend, and nearly had a heart attack. They wanted me to come home immediately, but I explained to her that Guy and I were in love, and had talked about getting married. We hadn't, actually, but I figured it was a logical next step. I wouldn't have done what I did if I thought otherwise. Not back then."

He hated the chill in her voice, the regret and the pain, and stepped closer, wrapping his arms around her, wanting to warm her, but she gently disengaged herself. Her eyes thanked him, but she kept herself separate while she continued her story.

"To make the story short, the news broke just after they left that week. I was studying for midterms, had my head in my books so deeply I didn't even know what had happened, why people looked at me the way they did when I walked outside, down the hall. I didn't find out until I'd gotten back that night from the library, and saw the college newspaper, heard it from friends."

Logan feared he knew what was coming next, and he felt sick.

"Turned out Guy had been caught running one of the largest college porn circuits in the U.S. It was a sort of game, an underground business run by chapters of various frats. They dated girls, took them back to their rooms, took pictures, hidden video, all kinds of things. Sometimes the victims were drugged, sometimes it was more like what happened with us. He had pictures of everything we did." She turned away, her voice too calm.

Logan's hands clenched with repressed rage. He wanted to kill this guy, even though it was probably ten years ago, but he couldn't stand hearing this. However, hearing it was not the same as living it, as Sarah had had to do. So he listened and waited. As much as he wanted to go to her, to hold her, he let her finish.

"They closed down the ring and the frat was under federal investigation. Guy was arrested and kicked out of school. All good things."

"He deserved much worse."

She nodded. "But in the process of the investigation, many of the photos were made public—a lot were already out there, floating around, as were the names of the coeds in them. The case was on the national news for several days, since it spanned colleges in several states. My pictures and my name showed up a few times. I was asked to testify, and I did. It just made it all the more public."

"Your family found out."

"Yes." She laughed a short, humorless laugh. "Everyone saw. But my family was crushed. They were so disappointed, so ashamed."

Logan could hardly believe his ears. "Why? Because you were used? Taken advantage of by that—"

"It was my fault. I let him do it, I was arrogant, going off on my own, not listening to them. Living in sin, having sex outside of marriage. In their eyes, I got what I deserved."

"You were a kid! They were your family. They should have been there for you."

"That's the theory. It doesn't work that way all the time. They prayed for me, so they said, but being together was impossible. I tried going home, tried to explain, to make it right, but saw nothing but shame in their eyes. Except for my grandfather. He understood. He stood with me against them."

"Good for him. What happened then?"

She shrugged. "I left school. All the counseling and political correctness in the world wouldn't stop the fact that people had seen those pictures, and it was the first thing they thought of when they looked at me. I had no social life—I mean, believe me, guys were interested after what they saw, but—"

He felt like a pig just being male, listening to what she'd been through. And it made him even more resolved to find out what had happened to Mel, to the other women who had been similarly humiliated.

"You went to Brooklyn?"

"Yeah. I'd always liked it there, and it was where Pops lived. He saved my life, I swear. He was the only one I had for a long time, the only one I could trust, and then when he passed…" She seemed to lose her breath for that moment, unable to continue, her back rigid and her head bent.

"You've done well for yourself. You've moved past it."

She turned then, her sad gaze catching his. "You never really get past it. That's why, on the beach that night, I couldn't, I wasn't able to—"

"That's understandable, Sarah. You were violated in a terrible way. It would be hard to trust."

She continued, not taking her eyes off him. "I tried dating a few times, but if a guy touched me, I just froze. I hated it. I wanted it out of my head, to be normal. I went so far as to force myself to go along a few times, even when it felt bad, and that was even worse, for them and me. The images from the tapes, the sounds, the feelings of being used, haunted me."

"Jesus, Sarah. No wonder you're gun-shy about sex. Who wouldn't be?"

"I can't shake the fear that the guy I'm with secretly knows about the pictures, or will throw them up in my face. Then, with my work, looking at so much…of that." Her hand drifted out, her eyes falling back on the pictures on the bed. "My sex drive just withered and died. And then there you were. Here you are. And everything is different."

And then she'd found a stash of porn in his dresser. Logan closed his eyes, realizing now why she'd looked like she wanted to kill him when he'd walked in the room. And why she'd been frightened—not that she'd admit that, but he could see it in her eyes. She'd thought he might hurt her, and it made him sick. He wanted to make sure she knew, insofar as it was possible, that he'd never hurt her. Never let her be hurt, not by his hand. He looked at her and tilted his face forward, resting his forehead against hers, cupping her shoulders gently.

"I'm glad, Sarah. I want it to be different with me. You can let go with me, I promise. I'll catch you."

She swallowed, tears swimming in her eyes and he pulled her in close, gathering every bit of her tightly against him. She was strong, stronger than anyone should have to be. She was tough and hard because life had made her that way, but he knew she was also soft, warm, vulnerable, and...*his.* It seemed quick to be thinking this way, but in his heart he knew.

He gestured to the pictures on the bed. "None of that has anything to do with us. It's ugly, dirty and demeaning. You and me, how we are together, we're nothing like that. What we have is...good. Clean. Amazing."

She looked at him, her heart in her eyes, and emotions swallowed him whole as she whispered to him, her breath caressing his cheek.

"Show me."

9

SARAH FELT uncharacteristically light as Logan ran his hands over her—free, unburdened by the thoughts and memories that usually plagued her. The sheer relief of knowing he wasn't what she'd feared, that he was truly one of the good guys, made the blood pound even hotter through her veins.

He'd been the only one ever potent enough to erase the images from her mind, chasing away her fears and driving her so blind with passion that she couldn't pay attention to anything but him. And now there was more than that. Now she knew she could trust herself with him, that he would take care of her. That when he looked at her—when he made love to her—he saw something good, clean and amazing.

She felt the goose bumps prickle over her skin, left in a wake behind the heat of his touch. Every nerve ending was on high alert, and she gasped when he bent his head, suckling her earlobe and then dropping his mouth to her breast, closing his lips over her soft flesh. Pulling her down gently, he set them both on their knees as he continued to worship her body in the most thorough, reverent way possible. She was shaking all over before long and had to plant her hands on his shoulders to stay upright.

When he lowered her back to the soft carpet and pushed the robe away until she was flushed and naked, she looked up at him, waiting. She'd never felt more cherished.

He was taut everywhere, his body straining toward her like an overstretched wire, but his eyes and his hands were gentle and slow. She arched when he slid over her, planting a hard thigh against her damp sex. He took her mouth in a plundering kiss, rubbing against her until she wanted to lock herself around him and ride him until she exploded.

But before she could, he moved away. Crouching, he reached out, lending her his hand. She took it as he pulled her upright, flush against him, kissing her breathless. She started to touch him, to do the things she knew excited him, but he caught her hands, folding them in his and bringing them up to his lips.

"Just let me love you, Sarah. Just let me make you feel good."

Her breath caught and she had no idea how to respond, what to do. What did he expect? Didn't he want her to touch him, too?

Tension started to pinch her neck, but before it could take hold, his hands were there, rubbing it away as he littered kisses all over her back and dragged his tongue up the length of her spine to the base of her neck, the tingling sensation making her shudder. He worked his way up and down every inch of her body, leaving no expanse of skin untouched, no shadowy crevice unexplored.

"Come here." His voice was low in her ear as he guided her toward a large divan by the window. He turned the light out, switching on a small dim lamp by the bed, bathing the room in muted golds. The window had been left slightly open and a cool ocean breeze wafted through it, making her shiver, the tight points of her nipples sharpening almost painfully.

"Logan…"

"Just relax, Sarah. Can you do that for me?"

She met his molten glance and was honest. "I don't know."

He took her by the shoulders, gently turning her over, returning his attention to her back.

"Close your eyes. Just feel what I'm doing to you. Don't think about anything else."

She was spread across the wide divan, her shoulders resting against the plump pillows that provided cushion next to the wall. Her skin was hot against the cool, soft upholstery, and she moaned when he slid his fingers between her legs, soaking them in the wetness he discovered there, and slicked it backward, massaging her in a way that had her fighting the urge to grind back against him.

"You're so beautiful, so strong… I love touching you like this…."

His mouth followed the wet path his fingers had drawn, and she cried out as he looped his arm under her belly and pulled her up, helping her balance as he separated her thighs farther then plunged his eager, hot tongue inside of her.

His large hands planted themselves on her bottom, holding her up and apart as he feasted on her, massaging her entrance with his mouth until she shook uncontrollably, her fingers digging into the satiny pillows as she rode out a shattering release. His hands were everywhere—on her legs, her clit, her stomach—the hot touches pushed the rolling waves of her orgasm to every point of her body, and she wasn't sure she could take much more. Her body, having lived too long with its needs ignored, was sure making up for lost time.

"Oh, please, Logan…" She panted, spent, whimpering when she felt him shift up behind her, his long, thick erection rubbing against her hip. She thought she couldn't take any more, but before she could say so he was inside her, filling her to the hilt. Reaching forward to grasp her breasts in both hands, he shifted her upright against him like a rag doll, thrusting inside her while he whispered sweet, hot things into the back of her neck.

It shouldn't have been possible, she was drained, exhausted, but the pleasure began to coil again and she braced one hand on the wall while curling the other back around his neck, drawing him in for a deep kiss, moving with him, tapping energy from some unknown depth.

At the last moment, when the sensation was too much, they opened their eyes, staring deeply into each other as they came, their sounds of pleasure intermingling as they pumped the last vestiges of pleasure from their bodies. Gazes still locked, they fell together into the cushions on the divan. She thought, somewhere in the back of her lust-saturated brain, that he had, as he'd promised, caught her.

"I SENT YOU on a damned vacation and you landed yourself in the middle of this?"

"It kinda fell into my lap, Ian. I swear. I wasn't working. It just…happened."

Ian sighed heavily on the phone, and she waited for the inevitable. She knew he'd react this way, but she also knew he wouldn't ask her to ignore what she'd discovered, or what Logan had told her.

"It's surprising what manages to 'just happen' to some people. So he has hard evidence?"

"He says."

"You haven't seen it?" Ian seemed a little distracted, and Sarah frowned, messing with the phone cord.

"We, uh, got sidetracked. But I'm heading down to his room now, and once I know more, we can figure out how to handle it."

"I'll wait to hear from you. And Sarah…"

"Huh?"

"Depending on what happens here, I still expect you to take some downtime when this is over."

"Yeah, uh, sure."

"I mean it."

"Yes, I know." She sighed, but before he hung up, she grabbed his attention once more. "Ian. Keep this close, okay? He's a good guy, and he's acting against orders, but, well. You know."

"I'll do what I can."

"Thanks. Hey, and congratulations. You know, on Sage. And the bun in the oven."

"How'd you know...? Never mind. Thanks, Sarah. Call me when you know more."

Sarah murmured a goodbye and hung up the phone, looking around to make sure she was alone. The inn was quiet; everyone had left for the morning. She peered up the stairs. She'd slept in Logan's room, slipping away quietly before he'd awakened to make her call to Ian.

She was glad she'd told Logan everything. They had something between them, something special, and she wanted the air clear between them. Telling him about what had happened to her, about Guy, had felt right, and had helped convince him why it was important for her to help.

She had feelings—more than tugs and shivers—real, punch-in-the-gut feelings that were growing for this guy. It may have clinched it that he was risking so much to help not only his partner, but the other women he didn't even know.

Sarah knew he'd also reached inside her and given her back a part of her life that she'd assumed had gone dead. She liked having it back. Suddenly, life wasn't just about work anymore. She was feeling things she'd never even known about, far beyond sex. And that was great, too.

For the moment, though, those feelings had to be set aside. She knew Logan had doubts, regarded her as a rookie and a desk jockey, but he'd find out differently. Together they'd solve the case, and then, well, they'd deal with what came later.

But for the first time in a while, she was thinking there was a future with a man in it, with the potential for so many things she'd thought she'd left behind for good. It was just wild.

Heading up the stairs, she hoped he wouldn't mind getting breakfast elsewhere and bringing whatever evidence he'd accumulated so they could go over it together. It was probably better if they discussed this outside of the inn. She tried the door, but found it locked, and rapped her knuckles softly against the wood.

No answer.

Frowning, she knocked again, and nearly jumped out of her skin when two arms slid around her from behind, laughing when she recognized the touch of those hands on her midsection.

"Morning, gorgeous."

"Morning. Where have you been?"

"I'd left a few things in your room—just retrieving them."

"Oh. Well, good. Since you're dressed, I thought we could go get breakfast downtown, and maybe talk about the case."

He moved past her, pausing for a second before he slid the key into the lock, and entered the room. Sarah followed, smiling at the sight of the pillows from the divan strewn all over the floor.

"Breakfast sounds good, but I don't think there's much more to discuss about the case. I told you everything last night."

"Just the bare bones. I have to see what evidence you've collected, and we can talk with Ian and E.J., come up with a plan—"

"Sarah," he cut her off, "I have a plan. I told you last night, there is no 'we' on this—I'll handle it. I don't want you involved."

Backing up, she took a breath. Clearly, they were experiencing a miscommunication of some sort, and she kept her voice calm. If they just launched into an argument, neither one of them would benefit. They were fighting the same enemy, they both wanted the same thing, to put these scum away.

"Logan, I told you last night why I am involved in this. For one thing, it's my job, and my jurisdiction. Second, I explained to you what happened to me, why it's important for me to help. And third, because I…" She lost her words for a second, looking into his eyes, searching for something that would encourage her to share her emotions with him. She did find warmth there—guarded by caution—and forged ahead. "I care about you. I want to help for a lot of reasons, but that's a big one."

He came toward her, wrapping her in his strong arms, squeezing tightly, then tenderly framed her face with his hands.

"I care about you, too. What's happening between us is obviously more than a fling, and that's why I have to say no. There's no way I am going to put you at risk. I've already lost too many people who are important to me."

"This isn't the same thing at all. Your family suffered

because of an accident. This is my job. Believe me, I'll be fine. We'll both be safer and more effective working together with the department behind us."

"This may be your job, Sarah, normally, but not this time. And jurisdiction doesn't mean squat in this case. I'm not bringing you with me, and that's that."

She moved slowly out of his arms. Her temper finally snapped—how could he be such a pigheaded, conde-scending jerk? "I'll thank you not to treat me like a child who has to ask your permission. I'm sorry you lost your family, but that's irrelevant here. You say you care about me, but you don't respect me enough to let me do my job. And besides, it's a done deal."

His eyes narrowed. "What does that mean?"

"I called my boss, told him what I found, told him what you told me—I assumed we were working to-gether, and he agreed we should pool resources to bring these guys down."

His eyes remained cool—in fact, they'd gone cold—and the tightening of his jaw signaled that he was furious.

"You *what?*"

"I think I was pretty clear. I called the head of our unit, and he wants me to review evidence with you, and get back to him to strategize. Don't worry, Logan—I told him the spot you're in with your department. He'll keep it to himself."

"So you went over my head? Even after I told you I wanted to do this alone? I didn't think you'd sell me out."

"You've got to be kidding! Sell you out? We're all ready to jump in and help you, you first-class moron.

Can't you see how much better it will be if you wait? If you work with us? Your chances of success will be much higher, and then it will look like we made the bust, clearing you with your department, and finding your partner's kidnappers."

"And conveniently putting a nice feather in your rookie cap while we're at it, huh? Very clever. But I already told you, I don't want the help, you were wrong to go over my head and I'm not strategizing with anyone. Period. In fact, I'm out of here today. I was hoping we could make some plans over breakfast, before I left, but now I can see that isn't going to work."

He turned away, and she took a deep breath, shaking inside, hating that he'd made her vulnerable, which made this hurt more than it should. His words had cut her to the quick.

"You said this thing between us, that it means something. That you cared—but you can turn it off so easily?"

He stopped, planting his hands on his hips, then shook his head.

"No. I can't turn it off. But I can't go on a case with you, wondering what's going to happen, worrying that you might get hurt, or worse. Wondering if I'm going to lose you by the end of the day."

Cold reality settled in her stomach and was reflected in her voice. She wasn't about to crawl out of here, hurt and shattered, at least not so he could see it. "Well, then I guess that settles it. There's no point in seeing what could have been, because nothing would ever come of this if you can't accept and respect what I do, and why

I need to do it. What did you think? We'd start dating and I would just quit my job for you? This kind of work will always be a part of my life. It's always been my life." *Up until last night,* she thought sadly.

He nodded, slowly, stiffly. "You're right. Nothing could come of this. I'm…sorry, Sarah."

She went toward the door, opening her mouth to say something, to let him know she wasn't about to back off from this case, regardless, and then thought better of it. Let him find out the hard way. She owed him nothing.

APPARENTLY, about thirty-five million years ago, a meteor—a big one—had come zooming out of space and smacked directly into the area that was now the mouth of the Chesapeake Bay, leaving a huge crater underneath the water as evidence of the impact. It had changed the shape of the sea floor, the direction of the rivers and the shape of the land as walls of water too large to imagine rose up from the impact and washed away everything.

Sarah looked out past the interpretive plaque that provided basic information on the Chesapeake Crater, and took some comfort from the breadth of the calm water stretched out before her. The Bay looked peaceful and smooth even though something had torn a big hole underneath it, destroying everything, altering all of the life around it forever.

She'd lived through the psychological equivalent years ago, and though she was feeling a similar impact from her argument with Logan, she wasn't about to let it destroy her. She could withstand it now; she was tougher, more experienced. She'd worked too hard to get where she was and she wasn't about to let a man crash down and wash away her strength, her life, her goals. No way. No matter if it did hurt like hell right now.

There was work to be done. She'd left the inn, gone for a walk to clear her head, but she was returning to Norfolk that afternoon to meet with E.J. and Ian. They were working the leads that she'd given them and she had no doubt they would quickly be up to speed on whatever information Logan had denied her. As if he'd thought she couldn't find out for herself.

Whenever people looked for information, on the phone or on the Web, they left footprints, and she knew exactly how to follow them. Her hacking skills, combined with Ian's clout and E.J.'s talents, meant Logan didn't stand a chance. Armed with that and with what he'd told her, it wouldn't take long to figure out the next step.

Of course, that was the long way of finding out what Logan was up to. The short way was to call Ian, tell him what had happened—that Logan was hotdogging it— and have Ian put a tail on him. See where he went and follow him there. And that's what she'd done. Logan wasn't going to get far without them knowing.

Later that day she was meeting up with E.J. and Ian at the office to go over their next move. She just hoped they figured it out in time to keep Logan from getting himself killed or thrown off the force. She understood his need to clear his partner's name and find out what had happened—she'd do the same for Ian or E.J., if need be—but it was his resolute rejection of her help that made no sense. And that was the part that hurt, too. Apparently he was only interested in her help in the sack.

As she turned away from the shore she stopped, hearing a choking sob. She listened more intently. Someone was crying. Was someone hurt? Perhaps there was a lost child?

Making her way down over a steep, sandy ledge she found the source: Ivy. Sitting on the wet sand, she was bent over with her face in her hands, her slight shoulders shaking.

She took a slow step closer, not wanting to startle the young woman.

"Ivy? Are you all right?"

Ivy looked up with tear-reddened eyes, misery carved into her features.

"Ivy, what happened? Are you okay?"

The girl didn't say anything clear as a yes or a no, but wailed something unintelligible, and Sarah sighed, squatting down in the slushy sand beside her, placing her palm on Ivy's shoulder to support herself as well as comfort.

"Ivy, talk to me. Why are you crying? Are you hurt? Can I help?"

Ivy took several deep breaths and seemed to compose herself.

"I'm sorry I interrupted. I just wanted to make sure you were okay."

Ivy reached over and grabbed her hand. Sarah waited for some more sobs to pass so she could speak. The young woman's hand was like ice, but her grip was strong.

"I'm sorry I just can't…seem to s-stop c-crying…."

"It's okay. Did something happen at work? Did you get in trouble? Were you fired?"

Ivy shook her head, biting her lip to choke back another sob, and Sarah realized the problem was personal as hot color flared in Ivy's cheeks.

"It's Jim," Sarah guessed flatly and watched Ivy nod. "What did he do? What happened?"

"W-we went out the other night. He took me for dinner, then on a nighttime paddle, and we ended up along this deserted stretch of beach. It was very romantic."

"Oh, God, Ivy. Did he rape you?" Sarah spun the young woman around, searching her face and hoping to God her first instincts were wrong. She felt the breath she was holding whoosh out of her as Ivy shook her head vigorously.

"Oh, no! No! We had a wonderful night, and we did, you know, f-fool around a little. He said I was different than the other girls he dated around here."

Yeah, right, Sarah thought to herself, but stayed silent. Guys hadn't come up with any new lines in decades. It was a shame the old ones still worked so well.

"So what happened, then?"

"L-like I said, we fooled around. I didn't mean to let things go so far, but he was so sweet. And I liked how it felt when he touched me. It never felt like that with anyone else. He asked me to trust him and I did—and it was amazing. I didn't know, I, um, you know." Ivy blushed furiously and looked out the sea.

Sarah didn't want to invite too many details—girl

talk wasn't exactly her forte—and nodded. "So what's the problem?"

Tears filled Ivy's eyes again, and Sarah started to feel impatience edge her mood—she'd had a crappy morning, and was looking at a long afternoon ahead of her. Now that she knew Ivy hadn't been physically attacked, she was anxious to get past the drama and move on.

"I went to see him this morning, to surprise him with some breakfast from the inn. When I got down to the dock, he was with some woman. He was kissing her. And not in the way you kiss your sister or friend, if you know what I mean."

Some temper flared in the girl's soft expression, and Sarah was relieved—temper she could work with. And it sounded like Ivy had every right to be angry. But she'd also been gullible, and now she was paying for it. Sarah knew that lesson by heart.

"It sucks to get burned like that, but he wasn't the right one for you. Men will say whatever they can to get what they want, Ivy, and you need to remember that. You can't just trust a guy because you have a crush on him, and you had warning about Jim. It could have been a lot worse than it is, and believe me, next time you'll know better."

Ivy paled beneath Sarah's harsh tone, obviously expecting more sympathy than she'd received, but Sarah was already standing. She may have been a little unfeeling, but she didn't particularly want to feel too much at the moment. Feelings just confused the issue and led to more trouble. She had things to do, more important things than dealing with Ivy's—or her own—bruised heart.

10

"SO WHERE IS HE?"

Sarah barged into Ian's office, pinning her gaze on the two men standing before her, expecting news. E.J. quirked a smooth eyebrow and made a tsk-tsk sound.

"Whatever happened to good manners? Hello to you, too, darlin'."

"Save it. I've been on the phone with you both all morning. We said hello hours ago."

"You modern girls. There's no charm."

"Yeah, like that's what you want with the hundred women you have in your PDA. Charm."

He grinned. "It sure doesn't hurt any."

E.J.'s easy teasing helped her tone it down a notch, but not by much. Ian was shaking his head, and began to bring her up to date.

"Logan checked into a motel on the beach, and left a little while ago to get some food, and then he stopped by a tux rental place," Ian related.

"He rented a tux?"

"Yeah, so he's obviously planning on attending some type of formal event. We have a list of all formal evening events in the area. His name's not on any lists, but he's probably using an assumed identity."

Sarah took the list. Something was off here.

"Where is he now?"

Ian drew in a long breath, and E.J. looked away. Sarah repeated her question. Finally, Ian gave.

"We're not sure."

"You *lost* him?"

Ian nodded. He looked tired, but that wasn't really new. Although life with Sage had tempered his workaholic habits somewhat, he still worked long hours, especially when they were active on a case. She backed down because she knew it would bug Ian more than anyone that they'd lost their lead. Her shoulders slumped.

"Shit."

"Exactly."

"Did you guys come up with any more from what I told you?"

E.J. nodded. "We have the woman, his partner, listed as staying at a Virginia Beach hotel before her disappearance. We requested the files from Baltimore."

"You let them know about Logan?"

"No. We just said we needed them as part of a larger investigation."

Sarah felt relief wash through her. She was pissed at Logan for a lot of reasons, but she didn't want to blow his career if she didn't have to.

"So what else do we have?"

"We know what room he stayed in at the motel. We're not sure if he made the tail at that point, so he could have felt safe enough to make some phone calls, or make some plans."

"Did you get into the room?"

"Not yet."

She looked at them, shocked. "How did you guys ever catch any bad guys without me?"

E.J. quirked an eyebrow at the comment—both he and Ian had been in law enforcement when Sarah was still in college. "Somehow we managed. But in this case, we thought you'd want to be in on it. If he made phone calls, maybe you can find out to where or to whom."

"I'd need access to the motel's computer."

"We could get a search warrant for that."

"That would take a while."

"Yep."

She pursed her lips, speaking the unspoken thoughts shared among them. "I'll need about five minutes alone with the desk computer."

Ian and E.J. grinned. "No problem."

A SHORT WHILE later Ian, E.J. and Sarah stood in the lobby of the small seaside motel. At its best, the place would be considered a fleabag. Hourly rates were posted and a sleazy little man sat in a swivel chair behind the sign-in desk, his head barely showing over the laminate counter. He peered at E.J. as he approached, Ian and Sarah staying back, huddled by the door, pawing each other suggestively.

"I need a room."

"Just you?"

"Uh-uh, the three of us."

The little weasel took his attention away from his on-line game long enough to smile in a sleazy, appreciative fashion. E.J. wanted to deck him right there.

"How long?"

"Three hours."

"Fifty bucks upfront."

E.J. peeled off the bills from an impressive roll of cash that had the little man practically salivating. It took so little to impress such people.

"I need room eighteen." He smiled conspiratorially. "My lucky number."

"Right. My lucky number is twenty."

E.J. peeled off another twenty, waving it in front of the man's beady eyes. He shrugged, handing him the key to room eighteen.

"Your money, pal." He looked over E.J.'s shoulder to where Sarah lounged against the doorjamb looking impatient and Ian leered at her convincingly. "Don't pull a muscle—she looks like a wild one."

"You can only imagine."

Within a few minutes they were in room eighteen, and though they searched the place thoroughly, there was no sign Logan had been there. Sarah turned to E.J. and couldn't help grinning.

"You make a convincing dirtbag when you work at it. Do you come to these places often?"

"Please, Sarah, you insult me. I only take women to the best hotels."

He looked down at the tacky clothes he'd picked up from the station's lost and found—he didn't really want to think too much about where they had come from—and ran a hand over his thick, sandy hair now slicked back with hair grease. None of the women he dated would touch him with a ten-foot pole looking like this.

"Will this stuff ever come out?"

"Sure. Just don't go for a swim or the EPA will be after you."

Ian glared at them, ceasing the teasing with an intense look in Sarah's direction—Ian was almost always intense.

"You sure you can do this? We won't have much time."

"You're kidding, right? Of course I can do it. All I have to do is hook into their PBX, find the numbers he called, if any, and we can do a reverse lookup back at the office. Piece of cake."

She pulled off her leather jacket, tossed her shoes away and stripped down to her bra and short skirt without blinking an eye. It was only Ian and E.J., after all. She smudged her lipstick with her fist and mussed her hair, leveling them a look.

"Uh, think maybe you should join me, here?"

E.J. wiggled his eyebrows lasciviously. "God, I love it when you go all Brooklyn."

They quickly stripped down to basics as well, and Sarah took a deep breath, grabbing a sheet while the guys did their part, wrecking the bed and breaking a lamp, and then turned to each other. E.J. smiled. "All in good fun. Remember, stay away from the face. I have a date tonight."

Sarah took a deep breath, wrapping the sheet around her as she went for the door, flinging it open, another crash sounding behind her as the guys did their part. She took off at a run for the office and burst in the door, yelling at the top of her lungs for help. A couple was signing in at the desk and stared at her wide-eyed. The scrawny man from behind darted out to face her.

"What the hell? What are you doing?"

Sarah gulped breaths, doing her best imitation of being panicked, and poured it on. Grabbing his shoulders, she let the sheet slip a little and watched his eyes dip, the worm.

"You gotta get up there, they're wreckin' the place, they're gonna kill each other!"

The smarmy desk clerk looked at her in confusion, then seemed to remember she'd come in with two men—she imagined short-term memory loss was an advantage in his line of work. Grabbing his shoulders, she pushed him toward the door.

"Go! I'll call the police! You aren't going to have a room left by the time they get done."

"Damn losers, come in a place and wreck it—I shoulda known when I saw you." He dove behind the desk, emerging with a baseball bat, and tipped it in Sarah's direction. "I knew *you* would cause trouble. Could tell the minute I saw you."

The other couple had already hightailed it out the door, and the worm followed behind. Sarah screamed at him about it not being her fault as she watched him go and then hurried behind the sign-in desk to the computer.

"Shit. Passworded." She didn't have time to try to figure it out, but had a hunch and lifted the keyboard, then
searched behind the monitor, and finally under the TV.
Nothing. But the sleazeball obviously had a hard time
remembering his own name, so he had to have it here
somewhere.

Taking out a slim drawer in the center of the beat-up
desk, she saw a small, ragged piece of paper with a
nasty acronym and what was probably his PIN number.
She shook her head.

"Dumber than I even thought."

She punched in the acronym, the screen freed and she
wiggled gleefully in the chair, her fingers firing over the
keys like a machine gun as she accessed the information they needed. Within minutes, she had the numbers—two calls had come from room eighteen last
night.

She hurriedly wrote down the numbers and shut
down the screen as she heard hollers and cursing just
before the clerk burst through the door again, Ian and
E.J. right behind him. He spotted Sarah.

"Hey, what are you doing back there? Get out of
there!"

She let her head sag to the side. "I was calling the cops,
moron. I couldn't reach the phone from back there."

He held the bat threateningly toward Ian and E.J., and
Sarah almost smiled. Her friends were under no threat
at all from the little man—either of them could put that
bat where the sun didn't shine within a hot second if
they wanted to.

"You two done fighting over me now? Maybe we can get down to having a little fun." She walked up to E.J. and dragged her finger down his chest. "Now that you're all worked up."

"You bet, baby." E.J. caught her by the waist and drew her close, winking at Ian. But the little man was having none of it.

"No way, you guys are freakin' crazy. The cops will be here, and you're paying for that room. I'm pressing charges!"

Of course, there were no cops coming. But he didn't know that.

E.J. loosened Sarah's hold and reached for his wallet again, bending his head down to talk with the clerk in a whisper. "Listen, I can't afford another arrest, okay? How about I pay you for the damage, let my girl get her clothes, and we'll take this party elsewhere?"

The clerk's beady eyes reflected his indecision as he looked at Sarah again, now draped over Ian, but then he caught view of E.J.'s wad of cash. He backed off, putting down the bat.

"Yeah, okay. Whatever. Give me the cash and get the hell out of here."

BACK AT THE OFFICE, it didn't take Sarah long to do a reverse lookup on the phone numbers. She was even more motivated to work fast because she was still wearing the hooker skirt she'd worn to the motel and it kept riding up far higher than she was comfortable with.

"Okay. I got it. He called Starline Cruises. Twice."

"That's a gaming cruise service. They run short trips, out past the legal boundaries, where state and federal gambling laws don't apply."

"That's legal?"

"Gambling is a big part of southern history—think of the Mississippi riverboats—and in this case, they don't gamble until they're far out on the water. So it's a loophole, but it works. There's a lot of it along the coast, some legit, some a cover for other operations."

Sarah sat silently for a minute, then snapped up straight in her chair, the pieces of the puzzle clicking together.

"Yes, that's it! I remember now, when I was arguing with Logan, he said something about how jurisdiction didn't matter. That's gotta mean he's out on one of those boats."

"Give me the number," Ian said.

Sarah and E.J. waited while Ian called, and he turned back to them as he hung up.

"He couldn't have made any trips today. The next one is tomorrow morning. He may be on that one. It's the next one out."

"I'm going." Sarah was adamant, and her partners looked at her curiously.

"Okay. But you're going in wired. You get in, see what he's up to, and let us know if you find anything. You'll be under constant surveillance," Ian said.

Sarah shook her head. "A transmitter's too risky."

Ian grinned like a kid. "Not the one I can get for you to use. Give me a few hours. Call and book yourself on tomorrow morning's boat."

Ian loved new toys, and she knew he was always keeping up with the latest in surveillance equipment. With his connections Ian often got his hands on things that few police departments could afford. He left E.J. and Sarah together and she reached for the phone, eager to get going.

It took her less than five minutes to make the arrangements for the cruise. Hanging up, she caught E.J.'s stare as he lay back in his chair, legs stretched out, his arms crossed over his chest, pulling the material of his suit a little tight at the shoulder. E.J. always wore suits to work. Expensive suits.

"What?"

"How did you find out about what Logan was up to? Doesn't sound like he was exactly forthcoming, and he obviously doesn't want our help."

Sarah closed her eyes and sat back in her own chair.

"He had some pictures. They fell out of an envelope when I accidentally knocked it off the table in his room. They were porn, and I nailed him, thinking he was either a consumer or a producer. He told me then why he had them. The rest is history. I told Ian, didn't he fill you in?"

"Why were you in his room?"

"What are you, my father?"

"Do I look like your father?"

"Maybe, thirty years ago. Especially around the eyes."

"You are such a smartass. So, you're involved with this guy?"

"E.J.—" Her address took on a warning tone, but he interrupted again, leaning forward.

"I'm just wondering. I'm concerned. You get a strange look about you when you say his name. When you talk about him. Not a look I've seen before."

"God, have you been watching *Dr. Phil?* I get a *look?*" She pursed her lips, repressing a grin. "Or are you just jealous?"

He rolled his eyes at her and she knew she wouldn't get him off the scent until she told him something. Once E.J. honed in on something, he rarely let go until he was satisfied. She threw her hands up.

"Okay, fine. I was in his room because, yeah, we had a little fling. That's all."

"Then it's over?"

"There wasn't any 'it' to be over. It was just a…thing." Her voice was flat and convincing, but it didn't stop the little dull ache the lie brought with it.

"I think it was more than a fling. You don't do flings."

"Why? Just because I didn't 'fling' with you?" She sat back, feeling pissed. E.J. had made a move on her shortly after he'd broken up with his fiancée. They'd just finished a case, she was a part of the team and they'd gone out for a beer together. He'd asked her if she'd be interested, and though she knew he wasn't looking for anything serious, she'd said no. Emphatically. She'd had no interest in getting involved with anyone, especially not someone she worked so closely with.

"Man, you get nasty when someone hits a nerve. But no, not because of that. Because I've never even seen you on a date. And now you're in this guy's room."

"Yeah, well, shows what you know. You have no idea

what I do in my free time." She was fussing with things on her desk, wanting to escape, when she felt E.J.'s hand on her arm.

"Sarah, if this guy means something to you—if there are complications—it could make the job dangerous. You know that. That's the professional reason I asked. The personal one is that I do know you, and I know that whatever happened out there, it's changed things for you, hasn't it?"

She acknowledged his question with a curt nod, but avoided eye contact. E.J. turned her around, made her meet his eyes. She hoped he couldn't see any more than she wanted him to, though somehow, he always did.

"Maybe you shouldn't be doing this."

"No, I am absolutely the one who should be doing this." She grimaced. Didn't anyone think she was capable of doing her job these days?

"I'll be fine. You and Ian will be hooked in the whole time. It's just reconnaissance, anyway. There won't be any action."

"You never know, Sarah. You know that."

"Okay, fine. Are you done poking around in my business now?"

E.J. leaned in to kiss her on her cheek. He was never put off, no matter how prickly she got. In fact, he seemed to enjoy it.

"You just be careful."

"I plan on it."

LOGAN MADE the tail before they could really know what he was up to, but it burned his ass anyway. He'd shaken it by slipping out of the motel through a back exit he'd located, and drank coffee for the three hours he had to waste until he caught a taxi to the docks. It wasn't like he was born yesterday.

Not only had Sarah gone over his head and reported his case to her superiors, but apparently they'd decided they were going to horn in on the case whether he co-operated or not. In the space of a day they'd gone from lovers to adversaries.

He was most definitely not cooperating. He had a good lead on them, and he'd used a fake ID to sign up for the cruise. As far as any of the ledgers showed, Karl MacKenzie was headed off for blissful two days of gambling at sea. He took just one bag with him, and most of the contents of his bank account. He didn't count on actually gaming all that much, but he had to appear like the genuine article, and that meant empty-ing his paltry savings to bring on the boat.

One phone call was all it had taken to find out which ship Mel had been on. He'd gotten the right person on the phone. She sounded young, and he'd put on his cop voice and asked for the information—which she never should have offered—but in two minutes he knew what he needed to know. One more call had him on board the same boat.

Reaching the boarding dock, he took in the shining sides of the sleek, white yacht. Its name, *The Gem,* was painted in gold-and-black script on the stern. Small sat-ellite dishes were placed at inconspicuous angles, and video cameras were everywhere. State-of-the-art security electronics, no doubt. And a sizable vault.

He walked forward and was greeted cheerfully by an older man dressed in a very expensive suit. Vince Valente, the boat's owner, most likely. He was then directed to a friendly young staff member who welcomed him aboard and offered to take his bag. Logan declined. He was directed toward his cabin, and Logan muttered his thanks, finding his own way.

It was a small boat, only accommodating up to a hundred passengers at any one time, but it was the top of the line in luxury and style. A very classy operation, at least on the surface. He wanted to find proof of what might be going on here under the glitz and gloss. And he had to work quickly. He'd only been able to afford the overnight package, and who knew if Sarah was on to him by now.

Walking down the narrow passageway, he skimmed past the ornate crystal hurricane lamps on the bulkheads and the artwork on the walls. He found his cabin number, slid his key card into the slot, and entered. It was a small cabin, smaller than your average hotel room but more luxuriously appointed. The bed was a double and took up most of the space. No television, no phone, no computer connections—no way for anyone to pass the time except for sleeping or gambling. He looked at the soft bed, and his thoughts went back to Sarah.

He knew she wouldn't give up. And part of him admired her for it, while the other part couldn't accept that she wanted to place herself in harm's way just to help him, or even to make peace with her painful past. He couldn't live with being party to putting her in danger.

He had nothing against women cops—Mel had been one of the best—but he hadn't been intimate with Mel. He hadn't cared for her in the same way. It hurt bad enough to have lost a friend, and Sarah promised to be much more than a friend. When she'd walked out of his room he'd nearly called her back, but he had nothing to say. He wasn't about to change his mind.

And now it was done. The tail they'd put on him had made it evident where her loyalties lay, and he accepted that, even if he didn't like it. He wondered if they'd contacted his captain. He was probably fired already, and that inspired even more of a feeling of recklessness. Sarah said they'd promised to keep a low profile, but that was when they thought he was cooperating.

Maybe he could have used their help—he wasn't even one hundred percent sure what he was looking for, or what he would uncover here. Even if the operation was used to trap unsuspecting women, they could be taking them back to the mainland to a filming studio or a warehouse where the porn was manufactured. His stomach rolled again, thinking of it.

He would just have to wing it—it wouldn't be the first time. He was here, he was on his own, and he was going to see what he could find. After a quick shower he dressed slowly, going over his game plan. Sliding his key card in his pocket, he exited the cabin and followed a group of formally dressed men and women up to the main deck. He was glad he'd rented a tux. Everyone was dressed to the nines.

He emerged into a space that stunned him for a moment with its grandiosity: bright light settled on rich mahogany tables, cream cushions on the chairs invited people to sit for just a little while longer, and a glittering bar dominated the port side. At the far end a buffet of expensive treats tempted him, the aroma reminding him he hadn't eaten much since leaving the inn.

He made his way to the bar, handed the bartender his key card, and ordered a beer. The little magnetic card did more than open your stateroom door. It also opened your credit card and cash accounts while you were on board. High-tech convenience and cash—it also meant customers ran up invisible expenses during their stay, and could drain their accounts without much effort.

He took the bottle and looked at the beer, sliding the glass back toward the bartender. Of course they only had the most expensive brands. It wasn't really a high rollers' club, but was geared toward making middle-class customers feel like part of the elite. Become part of the upper crust and suddenly you can afford to throw money around like them, too.

He turned as a cheer went up from an adjoining room—apparently someone was on a winning streak. The section he was in housed craps and blackjack. He made his way toward the food, planning to eat before he lost a little money, and then hopefully he could slip away unnoticed and start his search.

Hot and cold specialties were set before him on shining silver plates and crystal dishes. He would have been happy with a loaded burger, but he settled for a slab of prime rib.

Looking over the rest of the food, his eye caught something sparkling at the periphery of his vision. He followed the bait, catching a glimpse of smooth skin peeking through a slit in a glittering, cobalt-blue dress.

He admired the shapely foot at the end of the perfect calf, fitted into a heel that looked sharp enough to kill someone. Suddenly he understood why some guys liked their women to keep their shoes on while they did it. A husky voice spoke close by his ear, and he realized the wearer of the shoe was addressing him. He'd been caught peeking. She said only one word.

"Hungry?"

He closed his eyes, his grip tightening on his plate, then looked up. Sure enough, when he opened them, they were looking right back into the most wicked, beautiful blue eyes he'd ever seen.

"Sarah."

11

HE SHOOK HIS HEAD. "I should have known."

"Yes, you should have."

Sarah's tone was light, but her expression was neutral, giving nothing away. It was all he could do to manage the same. They didn't know who was watching.

She smiled, though the expression didn't reach her eyes, and he looked away, back at the food, relieved his voice sounded unconcerned.

"So how'd you figure it out?"

"Easy enough. Just traced a few phone calls—"

"From the motel."

She nodded and he shook his head almost imperceptibly. "I knew I should have used a pay phone, but I couldn't with your man on me."

"I was surprised you didn't shake him sooner."

"In my own city, in my own car, I would have. But time was short, and I had to get where I needed to go."

She smiled, hoping they looked like two singles meeting over the buffet.

"Let's eat and talk."

"I don't think so. You may be here, but I'm still working alone."

"Fine. Since you're not into working together, I guess I won't tell you what I've found so far."

She walked to a small, unoccupied table and sat down. She didn't invite him, but he pulled out the other chair and sat anyway.

"What you've found? You've only been here a few hours."

She reached over and tugged his tie lightly. "Stop growling and try to look like you're actually interested in me."

Something changed slightly in his eyes and he grasped her hand in his, rubbing his thumb across her palm, causing her breath to hitch.

"I am interested in you. You know that. That dress, by the way, is killing me."

She felt her cheeks warm—God, how long had it been since she'd blushed? She cleared her throat, easing her hand away.

"Um, you should know, we have company."

He looked around. "Where?"

Lifting her fingers to the onyx choker she wore, she spoke lightly.

"My necklace is a bug. Ian and E.J. can track me and hear every word I say, and every word said within about four yards."

His eyebrows raised, and he reached forward, sliding his thumb under the gold band, sending a shiver over her skin.

"I'm surprised they haven't picked it up yet—their security is tuned to find electronics that could be used for cheating."

"This is top-secret stuff—the shipboard system can't detect it. We're beta testing it for the feds."

"Cool." He leaned in closer, dropping his eyes to the soft skin of her throat. "Then your partners can hear me tell them to take a hike and stop trying to mess with my case."

She sighed. "Yeah, I'm sure they heard that, loud and clear. I'm also pretty sure they don't really care. This isn't just your case anymore."

His brown eyes glittered and he drew back, switching his attention to the dinner he'd been ignoring.

"So what did you find?"

"Oh, all of a sudden you want information from me? Pack sand. I'm going to go play."

She stood up, and his hand was like a whip, closing around her wrist and holding her still.

Heat flowed through her blood, temper and desire, and she fought equal impulses to deck him and to kiss him. It hadn't been long since those hands had touched her everywhere—and her body's responses leaped in remembrance.

"Hands off, Logan."

They were interrupted by a man who approached them, speaking quietly and politely. "Is there a problem here, ma'am?" The guy looked more like a bridegroom than a security guard, and Sarah decided within a second that she still wanted to try to get Logan on her side.

"No, I just want to go play, and my new friend…"
She looked at him engagingly, and he tipped his head
in acknowledgment.

"Karl."

She smiled brightly. "My new friend Karl is taking
forever to eat his dinner."

The man still watched Logan suspiciously. "The
buffet is available until ten, and after that you can special order anything you want from the kitchen until
2:00 a.m., sir, when the rooms close."

Logan smiled, thanked the man and walked to
Sarah's side. He wasn't hungry anymore, either way.

"I guess you're my date for the evening." His hand
settled at the bare skin at the small of her back where
the dress dipped low. "Karl MacKenzie, at your service."

She forced herself to concentrate on her job, and not
on his touch, but it was getting difficult. Logan had
shown her many new things about herself in the last few
days, and one of them was that she could apparently be
extremely angry with a man and still want him naked.

"What's your game?" He spoke casually, perusing
the tables.

"I've never really gambled. I never had enough money
to throw away. And you don't look at all like a Karl."

He just smiled, as if they were exchanging the most
fascinating conversation in the world. "Oh, they're
going to love you."

"I'm a quick learner."

"I'll bet. Why don't we start with blackjack? There's
not too much strategy to it, and it's fun."

Feeling contrary, she approached the craps table. She smiled brightly at the stickman, announcing cheerfully, "I've always wanted to try this, it looks like so much fun on TV—you know, I watch that Las Vegas TV show all the time, but they don't really tell you the rules. And there are all the odds to calculate, right?"

Logan rolled his eyes and stood by her side at the table. He saw the barely hidden smile of the guy running the table he knew he had a live one. As she listened to the rules, Sarah was all but jumping up and down with innocent enthusiasm. Everyone around her bought it hook, line and sinker. Logan had no idea she could be such a little actress.

Her talent—or lack thereof—at gambling only helped her case. She lost roll after roll, pouting prettily and handing the dealer her key card to load up again.

"Maybe we should change games, sweetheart? Your luck doesn't seem to be very good."

She smiled sweetly at Logan. "Hmmm. Maybe you're right. Let's try that blackjack thing you were talking about."

As they moved between the tables, Logan leaned down, whispering in her ear.

"You've lost about three grand, honey—how are you backing up all this debt?"

"It's going on a tab based on my credit card limits. Of course, it's a fake card number. A dummy account we set up before I got here. But if I'm guessing right, I won't have to worry about paying it."

"How's that?"

She smiled brightly, leaning over a little too far as she sat at the blackjack table, letting the dealer sneak a little peek. Logan closed his eyes and prayed for patience. He also prayed for a chance to slip out of here pretty soon and get some of his own searching done. Sarah, as usual, was botching all of his carefully laid plans. She gave the dealer her key card to get some chips, and chose her seat.

"Hey, sugar, spank me." She winked at the dealer and the young man looked like he was about to faint.

"It's 'hit me,'" Logan clarified.

"Same diff." She winked again, and looked at her cards.

Logan put in a bet and played as well. Losing, of course. However, Sarah actually won the next hand, and the hand after that. She was a quick learner. Logan played, watching her clap when she won and flirt outrageously with the dealer. He wondered if she noticed Valente standing in the corner. He'd been watching her all evening, making Logan want to stand in front of her, protecting her from the other man's gaze.

By the end of the evening though, Sarah had lost a significant amount of money. Logan was out quite a bit, too, though he was actually losing real money. Impatience and anxiety about wasting time and losing cash pushed his bad mood to the limit and when Sarah emerged from the ladies' room, he caught her elbow and pulled her into a dark alcove.

"Okay, we've established cover, and we're running short on time. I'm going to go see what I can find."

She shook her head. "The security's tight here—you won't find much before they notice you skulking around."

"So what do you suggest?"

She reached up, closing her fingers around his lapels, pulling him a little closer.

"Come back to my room."

"Sarah, this isn't the time—"

"I know. But I have this gut feeling about how things are working here. I draw attention to myself, look like I want some action. I lose a lot of money—maybe more than I can pay back, right? So maybe they have a way I can pay it back otherwise."

"By letting them film you?"

"Good guess. But I think they had me targeted as soon as I showed up on the boat."

"How can you tell?"

"My room is full of hidden cameras. High-fidelity video and audio that would never be noticeable unless you were looking for it. I looked."

"Do you think they made you?"

"No. I just fit the profile—single, female—the kind of person who might bring someone back to her room and give the perverts something to watch. They're probably watching in the meantime, though. The bathroom seemed safe. Thank God."

"I didn't even check my room."

"I don't think it's all the rooms, just a select few. But it's enough for us to bust them on invading privacy laws when we get back to shore, probably."

"I want them on more than that. They can swat a charge like that aside without breaking a sweat."

She stared at him intently. "I know. But maybe if you come back with me and help…bait the trap, I'll get an offer before long. If I take them up on it, I may get access to find evidence of what happened to those women. If I can just get near their computers, I can load a virus and hack in from the mainland when we disembark."

Logan hated to admit it, but she did have a good plan worked out, and it had a chance of working. The problem was that she was a prime target through the entire process—they could find out at any moment who she was or what she was up to, and he wouldn't necessarily be able to help.

"I don't like it. What am I supposed to be doing through all of this?"

"Keep an eye out and make sure they don't end up throwing me overboard."

"Not funny."

"I know. Sorry." She took a deep breath. "Wanna go back to my cabin and put a show they can't resist? I know we can get them, Logan. Trust me."

He wasn't ready for any of this. He didn't like it, but it seemed he had very little choice. If he wanted to find who'd taken Mel, Sarah was his best bet. And if she was going to have any backup whatsoever other than two guys ten miles away listening in, he was it. He took her hand, and just hoped she was right.

THEY HADN'T BEEN this awkward together since they'd met—although it had only been a little less than a week ago, so she didn't have too much to compare to.

As Logan hung back by the door, hesitant, his eyes filled with repressed desire and caution, Sarah knew she had to get him to loosen up. In spite of the tension between them, she knew he wanted her.

Throwing her wrap over the side of a chair, she went toward him. She heard his quick intake of breath as she pressed up close, planting a kiss just under his ear, and whispering.

"You have to take part in this. It won't be convincing if you stand by the door looking ready to flee."

He dipped his head, brushing his mouth over hers, then buried his face in her neck, and for a melting moment she wondered if she was going to be able to stay disconnected enough to get the job done.

"Where are the cameras?"

The words brought her back into focus—the idea of being taped zapped whatever desire she felt being close to Logan again.

"Over the bed in the light fixture, behind the bed in the picture frame, and in the dresser mirror."

"They made sure to get all the angles." He nipped her lightly, sliding his hand down to her backside and squeezing lightly, drawing her against him.

"We'll just give them enough to whet their appetite—we won't let things go too far. I know this is…hard for you."

"You have no idea."

He walked her backward toward the bed, taking control and kissing the daylights out of her. She felt as though she couldn't breathe as his arms tightened around her, his lips moving on hers like he was starving for her. She wrapped her arms around his neck, bringing every inch of her body in contact with his. The thin material of her dress was hardly a barrier against the heat and hardness of him, and she let herself revel in it. Logan tasted and felt like no other man alive.

His hand moved up to cup her breast and she arched into him. She had missed his touch. He murmured his appreciation against her lips and slid the shoulder of the gown lower so he could trace kisses over the skin there, and lower.

Sarah was barely aware that he was shielding her from the invasive view of the cameras by blocking any clear view of her body with his. She hadn't worn a bra under the dress, and when he tugged at a tight nipple with his teeth, she bit her lip to keep from crying out against the searing pleasure she felt, but a hungry moan escaped her lips despite her efforts.

He nudged her toward the bed until the backs of her knees hit the edge and she crumbled down to the bed. He lifted himself over her, shielding her from the camera eye above, but also parting her legs with his knee so he could insert his thigh against her, pressing intimately, rubbing his erection against her as he stared down.

She covered her exposed breast from view under the auspices of touching herself, and watched him stand, rip off his tie and slowly unbutton his shirt. She shivered, missing the heat of his body against hers, consumed with need as she watched him, but aware they couldn't let things go too far. This was just for show.

She hated that it was so easy to lose track, that her need for him was so strong. Wanting was one thing, needing was new territory. Dangerous territory.

When he knelt over her again, he reached down and slid his hands over her shoulders to her neck. Was he trying something kinky? She stilled, not understanding until she felt his fingers feeling for the clasp on her choker. She groaned again, though not from arousal—she'd completely forgotten that Ian and E.J. were listening in on the other side of the transmitter she wore.

Logan tossed the choker onto the chair by the porthole, hopefully far enough to be out of range. She didn't even want to think about what her partners had already heard. But it was all part of the plan, right? Logan whispered in her ear.

"Are you okay? Can you handle this?"

He was asking if she could handle their little scene, knowing they were being taped. To be honest, she hadn't even thought about it, and resented his bringing it up. She responded, licking his ear, her voice self-assured as she murmured, "Oh yeah…"

Then he was kissing her so deeply she trembled beneath his exploration of her mouth and wanted him just as deeply inside her. But they couldn't—not while being watched.

She slithered a hand down between them, massaging him through his slacks, and he pressed into her grip, his breath catching then coming faster as his arousal heightened.

"Maybe we should go back to my room." He suggested in a ragged voice.

She returned her mouth to his, whispering against his lips, "It would look suspicious to leave now."

He drew back, looking down into her face, studying her closely.

"Do you want me?"

"Yes."

"Tell me."

Meeting his gaze, she responded out loud, not needing to fake the desire in her voice. "I want you. Here. Now. Hard. Fast. However you want me."

She felt a sweep of satisfaction when he could no longer hold back the hunger in his gaze.

"I could use a shower first."

"Maybe I should join you."

"Sounds good to me."

She followed him to the bathroom, stopping before the door, sliding the dress from her shoulders and letting it hit the floor. She hoped the cameras didn't get a full view at this angle, and with no lights on, but they'd get enough. She picked up the dress, tossing it over on the bed for good measure.

"I'm all yours," she said seductively and followed him into the small bath.

"SHE TOOK the choker off." Ian's fist clenched and unclenched on the desk. Sarah was still unpredictable sometimes, and it riled him to no end.

"I guess she didn't want to get it wet," E.J. joked.

Apparently Ian was not in the mood for humor. And he was right. Sarah should never have put herself in a position where she took the choker off—it was their only link to her and what was going on.

"Did you know about this?"

E.J. sighed, closing the laptop now that the transmission was gone, meeting Ian's glare silently without so much as a flinch. They'd known each other for way too long and had been through way too much for him to worry about his friend's temper. Although it was never comfortable being placed between two friends, and he did feel loyalty to Sarah, he appreciated Ian's very real concerns.

"Sarah doesn't say much, you know that."

"Yeah, right." He sat back in his chair, reaching out to toy with an empty water bottle he'd left on the desk during their long stint keeping track of Sarah. "Funny, Sage and I always thought you two might—"

E.J. grinned. "I tried. She shot me down."

Ian quirked an eyebrow, his steely gaze still intent, but glazed with a bit of humor as he watched E.J.'s reaction.

"Why am I not surprised? But I can see why Sarah wouldn't want to be one of your flavors of the week."

"I'm wounded. But Sarah's not exactly the settle down and have babies type."

"Yeah, I used to think the same thing about Sage."

E.J. grinned, eager to change the subject. He was happy for his friends, but he enjoyed his life just the way it was. He'd been a slave to duty and responsibility for too long, and it could have ruined his life, always doing what everyone else thought he should do. Now he did what he wanted.

"How's Sage doing, by the way?"

"Good. As if she doesn't have a care in the world, still working ten hour days. She actually seems to have more energy than ever. Her consulting business is going like wildfire—no small thanks to all the recommendations you gave her, and to Grace's business."

"That's great." E.J. laughed, glad to know his sister had taken his advice and hired Sage. Ian was still scowling. "I take it you don't think that's great?"

"No, I do…and I don't. I don't want her pushing herself, and maybe something going wrong. Things can go wrong."

Though he enjoyed yanking Ian's chain whenever he could, E.J. also loved his friend and understood his fear. Back then Ian didn't know enough to really miss what he'd lost when his wife had miscarried. He knew now, though.

"You may be overcompensating a bit. I'm sure Sage wouldn't do anything she didn't feel up to doing. It's her baby, too, you know. You can trust her to do the right thing."

"I know. She's just so…stubborn."

"She has to be to deal with the likes of you."

Ian laughed.

"True. It's still so weird, to think of being a dad. I'd completely ditched that possibility. I just never thought about it again after what happened with Jen."

Pain and guilt still flickered quickly in Ian's eyes. Ian was not the kind of man to forget so easily, but sometimes he came on a bit too strong, worked a little too hard. He needed to ease back and enjoy what he had.

E.J. would probably be in Ian's position now, expecting his own first child, if he'd gone along with the marriage he had been supposed to enter almost a year ago. But he and Millie weren't meant to be married. It wouldn't have worked, a marriage based on friendship and familial expectations rather than passion and the desire to be together forever. He knew that now. And while he dated a long list of wonderful women whom he enjoyed and respected, he'd never met anyone who set him back hard enough to strap himself into forever with her.

E.J. smiled to himself. He was a romantic, to a degree. Part of his southern heritage. What was that old movie line? A head for business and body for sin? And a heart for love. That's what he wanted in a woman, too. But until he found it, he was just having fun.

Sage and Ian had the same kind of deep connection E.J.'s folks had had. In spite of their struggles, which all couples went through, they were perfect together. He hoped that whatever was going on with Sarah and Logan was something that would make her happy in the long run, too. She deserved it.

"E.J.—hello?"

He blinked, focusing back on the conversation.

Ian looked at him, stunned. "Wow, you were really zoning. I told you, Sage and I were going to wait to ask you together, I know it's still early, but I don't feel like waiting. We'd like you to be the twins' godfather."

E.J. leaned over and, clasping Ian's hand, pulled him into a hard hug.

"I'd be honored, man. Absolutely."

Ian smiled and sat back.

"We thought you'd be great. Just don't let Sage know I've already asked you—you'll have to act surprised later."

"Done."

"Okay, so now back to this." Ian gestured to the computer and E.J. knew his pal was like a bloodhound—he might have wandered off track, but he found his way back to the scent quickly.

"I don't know what's going on, Ian, and that's the truth of it. She's involved, but I don't know details. They have something going on, obviously, but she was tight-lipped about it."

"If they're lovers, it makes things even more hazardous than they already were. They're focusing on each other more than the threats around them."

"I think Sarah's sharper than that—she's come a long way—and this guy's experienced. You read his file?"

Ian nodded. "I also did some research into the owner of the cruise line. There's nothing solid, but he's been under investigation for crimes in South America and Southeast Asia. There's suspicion he's involved with black market prostitution."

"Providing Western women for sale abroad?"

"Exactly. The trails all seem to come to a dead end, no one's been able to nail the bastard directly, but he's potentially one very dangerous guy. Sarah could be sitting on top of a much bigger powder keg than she realizes."

"We should notify the Coast Guard, have them standing by just in case something goes sideways."

Ian's jaw tightened with purpose as he nodded in agreement. "Already done."

12

LOGAN TRIED to process what was going on—something didn't compute. He was naked. She was naked. She'd turned on the spray full blast, but instead of joining him for steamy, wet sex, Sarah was reaching for a towel and wrapping it around herself, hiding her delicious flesh from his view. From his touch.

His voice turned wary, "What's the matter?"

She closed her eyes, resting against the door.

"It was all for show, remember? I'm not really having sex with you, Logan."

He didn't respond, stunned, his skin chilling and his erection withering a bit. All that passion hadn't just been for show. She wanted him. She'd looked him in the eye and told him so, but even if she hadn't, he'd felt it. Felt her heat, her need.

Not sure what game she was playing, but not in the mood for it, he pinned her against the door.

"That was all just for show?" He lowered his head and grazed his mouth over her jaw, pressing against her so she could feel how aroused he became just standing next to her. "Really? This is only for show? It feels pretty real to me...."

He reached between them and tore the towel from her body, desire coursing through his veins as his hot flesh came in direct contact with hers. He moaned, burying his face in her shoulder. He inhaled her scent, tasted the soft skin there and felt her shudder.

There was nothing false about what they were feeling, he thought with satisfaction. Her nipples jutted against his chest, hard, begging for his attention, which he would give them as soon as he finished with her lips. He was obsessed with her mouth, and settled his own over it, urging her to comply. Though her hands were on his shoulders as if to push him away, she didn't.

Exploring deeper, nudging his erection between her thighs, he felt his temperature rise unbearably, but in the back of his mind something niggled at him.

Her hands hadn't moved, remaining still on his shoulders. She didn't push him away, and she let him kiss her, let him touch her, not denying her own response. But she didn't make love back to him. She was letting him take, but she wasn't giving.

He took a step back, looking up into her face. Her skin was flushed with passion, but her eyes were filled with sad resolve.

"You said you wanted me."

"I do want you."

"So why the chill?"

"I don't like being used." She held up a hand to his mouth, covering his lips gently as he started to object.

"I know it's not how you mean it, but it's the end result. Being together, working on the case, having to set up a sting—it gives us a neat excuse to go further, but we shouldn't act on it."

"Why the hell not? I want you, you want me—we can be relatively sure no one's watching in here, so what's the problem?"

She smiled a little, and it actually made her look even more sad, which made it hard for him to breathe. He knew almost before she spoke and sucked in a deep breath, getting control of himself. She was right. He'd totally lost his focus about why they were there. He should be thinking only of finding Mel, and hopefully the other two missing women. They had a job to do, and he had let it go completely in his pursuit of Sarah. He shook his head in disgust with himself, and then looked up to meet Sarah's eyes as she spoke.

"Where are we heading, Logan? What's next?" She bent to pick up the towel. "What is this? What am I to you? I thought we laid things out pretty clearly back at the inn—you don't respect my job, don't like what I do."

"I don't like you putting yourself in bad situations. And this is one—I'd lost track of that for a few minutes, and I have to apologize." His voice had turned stiff, and he just wanted to have this over with; it was all getting too complicated.

"But danger is part of my job. Not every day, but when I need to deal with it, I do. I don't—and can't and won't—sit behind a computer all day and let other people go take the risks. That's not how it's done. That's not who I am."

"I just can't stand the thought of you getting hurt."

"Just because your mother and sister got hurt, just because Mel got hurt, doesn't mean I will."

"You could."

"So could you—it doesn't mean I would ask you to be less than you are. If you really cared for me—wanted more than…" she sputtered, gesturing to her naked body beneath the towel, "more than *this,* then you wouldn't ask me to give up who I am, either."

He sagged back against the opposite wall, desire erased, misery setting in. She was right. But it didn't necessarily matter.

"I don't know what I can do. I just don't know, Sarah." His emotions were raw in his eyes. "What I do know is I don't want to lose you. How can you blame me for that?"

She looked away, her beautiful lips set in a flat, painful line as she maintained her control. "I think we've been in here long enough for them to buy it. You can go back to your room now."

The distance she put between them with the statement was tangible, and he nodded. He wasn't about to beg her for what he wanted.

His voice was neutral. "We'll have to get wet. They need to think we were showering."

"You first. I'll follow after you leave. They can think we said our goodbyes in here."

His heart ached. Maybe they had.

As SHE LEFT her cabin the next morning, feeling all the

worse for wear and hoping it simply looked like she'd had a late night partying, she wasn't completely surprised to be detained by a yeoman.

"Ms. Jessup. If you could come this way, the owner of the ship requests the honor of your company at breakfast."

"The owner? What would he want with me?"

The yeoman smiled. He seemed younger and more innocent than he must surely be, Sarah thought. Did he know what was going on, or was he just another dupe?

"On each trip, certain guests are invited to join Mr. Valente for breakfast on the last day of the cruise. Such an invitation has been extended to you."

"Oh, well, I suppose that's quite an honor. I can't imagine why he would choose me. Perhaps I should change into something more suitable…." She presented a flustered, nervous facade, and the yeoman smiled, taking her by the arm. No, he wasn't about to let her walk away. Definitely part of the pack.

"You're perfect just as you are. Mr. Valente will not want to be kept waiting. Come this way, please."

She tried to squelch the excitement that her plan appeared to have worked. Logan was nowhere in sight, but she did have her choker on, so she wasn't alone. She stepped up into a grandly decorated room that occupied most of the space under the bridge and was left alone as the yeoman closed the door behind her.

A table was set with a breakfast that smelled like heaven. Regardless of the fact that it was bait meant to draw lambs to slaughter, she was starving. There were also only two chairs—so much for the yeoman's story about the owner inviting several guests to breakfast. She was the only special one, apparently.

Unable to resist the grumbling of her stomach, she grabbed a croissant from the table and walked casually around the room, looking for anything that might lend a clue to the seedy operation they had going on here. Not that she expected anything to be just lying out in the open, but it was possible.

She turned when she heard a door open on the other side of the room, and saw a man enter. He was in his fifties, she guessed, and not bad-looking for his age. Kept himself in shape. He was dressed in a casual business suit, his salt-and-pepper hair long enough to be youthful but neatly groomed in a way appropriate for his age. His blue eyes mirrored hers, and he smiled with perfectly straight teeth.

"Ms. Jessup. So nice to see you could make it. Please, have a seat. I see you already started without me."

"Sorry. I was hungry." She offered a smile, and he returned it, waving her apologies away with a careless gesture.

"You should feel free to help yourself. You're my guest."

Or your prisoner? she wondered. How long would he bother to keep up the little play they were engaged in? She decided to string it out, get him to talk, and sat, starting on a cheese omelet. It was going to take some energy to kick this guy's butt. They made small talk for a while, and she began to get restless.

"Thank you for the breakfast and conversation, but I

need to go. I'd like to get some time in at the tables before we get back to shore."

"Please, please. Relax. You have plenty of time, several hours before the tables close. I can't possibly allow you to leave just yet."

"But I want to go."

And there it was. She noted the flicker in the eye, the mean little twitch in the cheek that belied the suave charm he'd been pouring on. She'd pressed the right button—a guy like him wouldn't like a demanding or stubborn woman. She needed to tread carefully, to play him out and get him to say as much as possible, the little recorder on her neck carrying everything back to Ian and E.J.

"I don't think so. We need to talk."

"About what?"

"I want to make you an offer."

She pretended to be curious, and sat back in her chair, though she didn't touch her food.

"What kind of offer? I already have a job…."

He smiled, and it was smarmy and condescending—they'd no doubt looked into her background. She kept her own name; using a fake name was asking for trouble on such a short job, when she didn't have time to get used to a new identity. But she'd trumped up a background as a full-time waitress in a swank seafood restaurant where she did fairly well. They'd also made sure she appeared to have a bit of a gambling problem.

"Yes, we know about your work. And we know about your debt—including the debt you accumulated last night. I know you don't have enough in your credit account or your bank to cover the losses, Ms. Jessup."

"How can you know these things about me? You have no right—" She was enjoying her role as the outraged woman, the nervous gambler in too deep, and played it to a tee.

"I have every right. I know everything about everyone who sets foot on this ship. I know everything about you."

He leveled an intimidating look in her direction, and it was all she could do not to spit in his face and tell him how stupid he really was. But, as she'd learned over the last eighteen months or so, that wasn't the best way to get the bad guys. She controlled her temper and swallowed her disgust.

Sarah let her voice quaver a little as she responded. "I promise I can pay my debts. I always do. It'll just take me a little time, maybe some payments…?" She looked at him hopefully, and watched the sick satisfaction in his smile when he thought he had her where he wanted her.

"We don't really do payments. But there are a few other arrangements we can make. If you are willing."

Yeah, sure, and probably even if I'm not.

She licked her lips and swallowed, eager to get specifics, but coming across as hesitant.

"What kind of arrangement?"

Valente stood and walked around the table, standing behind her, though he didn't touch her. She looked back over her shoulder questioningly, but didn't turn around.

"There are customers we have, wealthy clients, who

come to play and are unattached. They would enjoy some female company while they are here."

"You mean, like a date?"

"Exactly. They are usually foreign businessmen, traveling abroad, and they have certain…preferences, shall we say, for American women. Especially attractive ones like you."

He actually felt he'd paid her a compliment, she thought with disgust. Valente walked to the side of the table, leaning his hip on it slightly, and reached down to push a little hair back from her forehead. She let him, while fantasizing about breaking his fingers.

"What would I have to do? Would I have to come back?"

"You could take care of your obligation immediately. Tonight."

"But I'm due back—"

"Change your plans." He bit out the phrase, and she shrunk back.

"I don't know about this. I don't like it. I just have to keep them company while they're playing?"

"Yes. Though if they want more, you shouldn't argue."

"You mean you want me to have sex with them? For money?" She raised her pitch into an indignant squeak and pushed up from her chair.

"Sit back down, Ms. Jessup."

"I am not going to have sex with some nasty old foreign guy. Forget it. I'm outta here."

"You are staying right where you are."

"I told you, forget it."

She headed toward to door, waiting to see what else he would do.

"You may want to see this before you go. It was taken last night, and would be sent to your employer, your family—and anyone else we think might be interested."

Sarah let her hand drop from the door, and turned slowly as she heard Logan's voice up close—the recording was much better than she imagined it would be, and she didn't have to feign repulsion as she watched Valente smirking as Logan pushed her dress down.

Luckily, Logan's moves had blocked most of the view of her exposed skin, but still. It was obvious what was happening between them—the sex, the heat between them, jumped off the screen. You couldn't see his face, but her identity was clear. Her stomach turned for real, her past rushing back to her in a oily stretch of disgust. She pushed it down. She had to focus.

"Yes. We have the entire episode, and our video people can easily enhance it, livening it up where the action got a little…slow."

"You wouldn't! This is against the law, I'm going to tell—"

He grabbed her by her shoulders, hard. She winced, reassuring herself that Valente wouldn't want to damage the goods. If he did, she could take care of herself until help arrived.

"You will not breathe a word of this to anyone, you stupid, penniless tramp. Do you understand? You will do what you're told, when you're told to do it. And if you do a good enough job, maybe your debt will be paid in full." He glared at her ominously. "If not, you will be at my disposal until I feel your debt has been worked off."

She gave in and spit at him, feeling real tears born of anger stinging behind her eyes. She struggled to get out of his grasp.

"I'll throw myself overboard to the sharks before I'll stay here with you!"

"That can be arranged as well. But not yet."

He let her go roughly and hit a button on a panel near the table, never taking his eyes off of her. Sarah gulped huge breaths he would no doubt read as fear, but it was really her need to control herself and her anger so as not to rip him limb from limb.

He'd threatened to kill her, if necessary. Is that what had happened to Logan's partner? She was a cop, too— a tough woman who would never have given in easily to something like this. She listened to him call someone, and a moment later the yeoman stepped through the door.

"Take her to the lower stateroom. Make sure she doesn't get out."

"Yes, sir."

"I won't go! Get your hands off of me!" She kicked out at the yeoman and was rewarded with a fist to the gut, knocking the wind out of her. Valente nodded approvingly.

"Yes, don't bruise her. Visibly."

Sarah muttered more curses and let the yeoman drag her from the room, catching her breath as she went and hiding a slight smile. Now she really had the bastard exactly where she wanted him.

"CAN YOU GUYS HEAR ME? Send me a feedback signal so I know you're out there."

Sarah sighed with deep relief when the answering sound of a whining pitch made her wince. She wasn't cut off. Locked in a room and lying on the small bed, she hid her head behind a pillow, appearing to sleep while whispering into the mike still secured around her neck.

The room was actually very comfortable—she'd thought they might throw her down in the engine room, or whatever the equivalent of a basement was on a boat. Now that she knew Ian and E.J. could hear her, she started formulating a plan.

"Okay, I'm going to need Logan on this one—you guys need to find a way to contact him here and let him know where I am, what's going on. I'm going to see what they do with me later—I'm betting they won't take me up where all the other clients are and risk me making a fuss, so I imagine whatever plans they have for me, they'll be doing something private."

She grinned for a moment, imagining Ian's frustration at only being able to listen and not talk—he must be going crazy, and the thought tickled her a little. This is what he got for sending her on vacation. But she was in the driver's seat now, and she was going to make it count.

"I know we have enough to bust them on now, but don't you dare send the cavalry in just yet, Ian. I mean it. I want to nail this guy in a big way—we need to find the missing women Logan mentioned. They could be on the boat, or we could at least find out where they are. We need to get access to their computers...."

Her mind started clicking away as she mumbled into the mike, telling them what she needed and what she was planning to do. Her heart beat a little harder in anticipation of snagging Valente and uncovering the full extent of his activities. As long as Logan came through, they'd be all set.

LOGAN STARED OUT the aft window. Everything in his life felt frustratingly out of his control—the investigation, his emotional responses toward Sarah, his job.

He'd been awake the rest of the night, tossing and turning due to stifled desire for Sarah. He could work with women cops, stand beside them on the front lines as he had with Mel, but he didn't know if he could be in love with one. As if he seemed to have any choice in that matter, either.

Sarah hadn't come up yet. He glanced at his watch, worrying. If she didn't show soon, he'd go after her, whether she liked it or not. They would only be on the ship for another twelve hours or so—they were heading back to land that evening. He only had one shot at helping Mel, and he had to take it soon. After he left this ship, there was a chance he'd never know what had happened to her. His jaw hardened at the unacceptable thought.

He turned toward the stairs to go find Sarah, and

nearly slammed into a member of the staff who stood before him, handing him a small envelope.

"Telegram for you, sir."

"Are you sure you have the right person?" Who would be sending him anything?

"You are Mr. K. MacKenzie?"

He took the telegram, frowning. No one else knew about his alias except…he took a deep breath, realizing.

"That's me. Thanks."

He tore open the small envelope and tried to decipher what the heck was on the inside. The name Ian Chandler stopped him in his tracks—Sarah's boss. His breath came up short, realizing that Sarah must be in trouble.

TO: Karl MacKenzie
FROM: Ian Chandler
RE: URGENT BUSINESS
Critical meeting has been detained. Urgent contact at 555-8888 to reschedule immediately.

Logan looked around. Much like with airplanes, cell phones weren't allowed on board because of terrorist threats, and the only phones were in staff offices and on the bridge. He had to get to one, fast. He looked around for the young woman who had delivered the message and approached her, smiling as charmingly as he could manage.

"Ms. Simpson—" he spotted her name tag just in time "—I have some urgent business to attend to. I wonder if you could show me to a telephone?"

She looked up into his face. "Ship-to-shore calls are very expensive—your account would have to be directly billed."

"Of course. But this telegram is about a problem that must be settled this morning."

"Of course, sir."

That was easy. He was led down the stairs to a narrow hall where doors seemed more compact—staff quarters and offices, probably. She led him into the small, crowded office and he tried not to pounce on the telephone too eagerly.

"I should just be a few minutes, I think."

"We can't leave any offices unattended, sir, for security reasons. I'll have to stay in the room."

Logan flatted his mouth disapprovingly, but nodded. It would cause less suspicion this way, anyhow.

"Fine. Glad to know you run a tight ship."

He dialed the number, and waited as the slow connection made its way through. The line was somewhat fuzzy with static, but relief overcame him when someone picked up on the other end.

"Ian?"

"Yes."

"It's Karl. What've ya got?" He assumed a casual familiarity with the stranger on the other end of the phone—it wouldn't exactly be convincing that he had urgent business with someone he didn't even know.

"Logan, are you alone?"

"No."

"Okay, then just listen. We've tested this line, we're

scrambling, but I'm going to make this quick. Sarah is locked in a cabin in the lower stern—they're holding her there. She's okay, and we're keeping track of her. We need your help, though."

"Sure. Tell me what you need to make this happen."

"We need to do two things—get Sarah out of there safely, and get into their computers before we send in the Coast Guard. They'll wipe their systems if they suspect anything or know they are being boarded, so we need to get into their network first and download as much as we can before we raid."

"What's my part in all this?" Logan looked up and saw the staff member leaning by the door, looking at her fingernails while he spoke. She didn't seem to have any particular interest in his conversation. Good.

"We're going to make a drop later this morning— we have someone on the way now. The Coast Guard is going to pass by, do a routine check. The cruise lines expect this, so it won't be suspicious. They'll send out a diver who'll leave a small package attached to the stern. In that package you'll find a receiver, so you can communicate with us, and a small computer card."

Ian took a breath, then continued. "Here's the hard part. You need to get that card attached to one of their main computers—Sarah said she saw one in the room they took her to this morning, Valente's cabin. Just slip the card in the slot on the side or in the back of the computer tower and leave. Then we'll locate Sarah, and you can get her out. When they're being raided, they won't hesitate to get rid of her, or any other witnesses. You need to get to them beforehand. Got it?"

"Yeah. I'll be in contact."

He hung up, shaking his head. He'd felt as though he'd stepped through the looking glass as soon as he'd arrived at the inn, and things had only gotten crazier. All these secret transmissions, coded messages and things being attached to the sides of boats. In his other life, police work was never this complicated. It was a lot of footwork and a lot of paperwork, and he did his best not to get shot. All this James Bond stuff was unfamiliar, but if it worked, it was fine by him.

They had Sarah, and while the thought made him sick, he had to cool down and trust that she was okay, that she could handle herself. Chandler had a trace on her, and they had backup waiting, so all he had to do was get the card in the computer and get her, and whoever else was being held—maybe Melanie—out.

That's all.

He walked through the gaming room, trolling the tables as if deciding which game to play, figuring out his next move. There wasn't much he could do until he had that card in his hand. Anticipation of seeing the Coast Guard vessel draw alongside buzzed through his bloodstream, but he saw nothing on the water just yet. He glanced at his watch unobtrusively, returning to the craps table to watch the early rollers.

He realized that the resentment he'd felt at having control over the investigation taken away from him had suddenly evaporated. The short conversation with Ian replayed in his head. Logan had thought he wanted to go it alone, but he had to admit it was good to be part of a team again, ad hoc as it might be. It was a feeling he'd missed since he'd lost Mel and been on the outs with his own department.

And whatever it took, he was going to make sure he didn't let Sarah down. Regardless of what the future did or didn't hold for them.

13

SARAH WAS LYING silently on the bed when Valente walked in, eyeing her with displeasure.

"You should be dressed and ready by now."

She continued to stare at the ceiling. "I told you, I'm not going to do it. I don't care what you do with the tapes."

He opened the door again, and whispered something. Out of the corner of her eye she saw more movement, and a large man came in behind Valente. He had a gun. A large gun.

Sarah didn't move until Valente grabbed a fistful of her short hair and yanked her up. She bit back a whimper at the stinging pain, glaring at him. Bastard.

"You will shower, you will dress in the clothes I have provided, you will make yourself beautiful and do everything you are told without argument, or Lex here will have some fun with you. Before he kills you." He tugged her head back, forcing her to meet his eyes. "Are we clear?"

"Very."

He smiled. "Good." Then he removed his hand from her hair, moving it to her throat. He ran his finger under the chain of the choker, grimacing. "This is cheap. You can't be seen in this." With a sharp pull he ripped the choker from her throat and she grabbed for it.

"That's mine. It has…sentimental value."

Valente dropped it to the floor, stepped on it, and smiled widely at the crunching sound under his heel.

"Be thankful it was the necklace and not your neck."

With that he left the room. Sarah looked Lex the gorilla in the eye, wondering if she could take him. Probably only if she could get his gun away from him. He let his eyes wander down her body lasciviously. Snatching up the clothes, she locked herself in the bathroom.

Without the choker she was truly on her own. If they took her somewhere else, or threw her overboard, no one would know. Hopefully Ian and E.J. had contacted Logan, and they were on it.

Help would be on the way soon, she reassured herself as she stripped, self-conscious even though she was alone in the shower stall. She hoped she could stay alive and unharmed until it arrived.

LOGAN WAS going broke as he ordered another whiskey from the bar while he crapped out yet again at the table. The guy next to him slapped him on the back in condolence before he left with a woman who'd only spared Logan a look that said "loser." Well, it was the image he was working to project.

Good. As he took a sip of the whiskey, then covertly emptied the rest into the plant that sat next to him at the table, he figured his plan was working. The Coast Guard vessel had shown up, run alongside and done a visual inspection from their ship—while a diver left the computer card. Logan had surreptitiously retrieved it while taking a break from his losing streak. Now it was time to try to get into Valente's office.

Pretending to down the drink, he slammed the glass back down and set both hands on the table, snarling at the stickman.

"I've never lost this much in my life. This game is rigged!" He raised his voice, slurring his words just a little. The man by the side of the table looked offended and raised his eyebrows.

"I want my chips back! This guy should be replaced. This table is a rip-off."

Logan wasn't surprised when a very large man in a dark suit appeared by his side.

"Is there a problem, sir?"

Logan turned and faced the security guy, practically nose to nose.

"Yes, there's a problem. Cheating is a problem."

"I can assure you there is no cheating on this boat. Maybe you should let me see you back to your room."

The man grabbed his shoulder in an iron grip, but Logan had no problem shaking him off. He could probably take the guy, but his real goal was to grab the attention of the big guns, and if he had to take a punch to do it, he was up for that.

"Get your hands off me, flunky. I want to talk to the owner of this cruise. I want to talk to the captain!"

"Sir, you need to quiet down…." The ape's voice had taken on a more threatening timbre now, and Logan saw his real opportunity. He pushed out, shoving the guard back.

"I will not be quiet. I demand to see the owner. I am not going to deal with some—"

Someone slid between them, narrowly saving Logan from a black eye or worse. He confronted a man of about his own height, though of a slighter build, in a very expensive suit.

"I'm Vincent Valente, the owner. You have a complaint, sir?"

Logan huffed out a breath, giving the man the full effect of what whiskey he'd sipped. He watched him grimace in distaste, and did it again before he spoke.

"You're the owner?"

"Yes, I am. I overheard you wanted to talk with me?"

"Yes, I do. I keep losing at this table—I think it's rigged. I want proof this table is not rigged."

Valente slid a look to the side as some other customers approached the table and then discreetly walked away. Returning his hard gaze to Logan, he tried to appear friendly. Logan could see he was anything but.

"Well, why don't we go back to my cabin where we can find a resolution to this issue?"

Logan smiled a drunken smile and grabbed Valente's hand, shaking it hard. "That would be very good, yes, very good. I knew if I could just talk with someone in charge, things would work out."

They hurried him out of the room, Valente making chitchat along the way. Everything seemed pleasant and professional enough—maybe too much so, Logan thought uneasily as they approached a door at the end of the hall.

He was glad he'd thought ahead and slipped the card in his shoe, and placed the tiny transmitter in an inside pocket where it hopefully wouldn't be detected. It looked like a watch battery. Sarah's cohorts had some seriously advanced toys. If his escorts found it, they probably wouldn't realize what it was. He hoped.

The door opened, and before he could brace himself, he was roughly shoved into the room. He stumbled to the floor, and it occurred to him that he might not have avoided that bruising after all. He picked himself up slowly, still maintaining his inebriated behavior. Holding his position on all fours for a second, as if disoriented, he looked up and spotted the computer desk at the far side of the room.

But before he could get up, a foot caught him in the stomach, knocking the breath out of him and sending him slamming over onto his back. He gasped for air, not needing to fake a thing in his pained response. He looked up to see the security guard towering over him, eyeing him like a big dog getting a treat.

Logan pushed himself up into a sitting position, groaning. "What the hell? Is this how you treat all your guests?"

Valente smiled pleasantly, staring down at him.

"No. Only the ones who accuse us of cheating."

Logan held up a peaceful hand. He had to find a way to get back by the computer.

"Okay, okay. I'm sorry. I just lost a shitload of money, that's all. Can't a guy be pissed?"

Logan raised himself up and staggered forward, holding his gut, feigning a sheepish expression.

"No, not when it could cause irreparable damage to my reputation."

Logan nearly laughed out loud, but staggered a little closer.

"I said I'm sorry." A little closer....

"Your apology is useless. You are banned from any of my gambling establishments Permanently. Call yourself lucky."

And just close enough. "Why, you filthy…" Logan jumped forward before any of them could see what he was going to do, and he pounced on Valente, landing one hard punch to his jaw. Valente's head whipped back with the impact, but he was tougher than he looked. He didn't go down. Instead, he spoke calmly to the guard, but there was violence in his eyes.

"I have a meeting to attend. Apparently, Mr. MacKenzie didn't get your point—make sure he does."

The guard grinned at Logan, practically salivating. Logan circled the room, bracing himself to take some hard knocks but positioning himself so he'd take them in the direction of the computer.

"Be quick about it. Then get back out on the floor." Valente muttered the warning as he opened the door, wiping a little blood from his lip.

When the door closed behind Valente, Logan sharpened up—no need to let himself get beaten to a pulp now that he was alone with Valente's goon. He smiled sharply as the guard's Neanderthal brain slowly figured out that Logan wasn't drunk at all.

Logan stretched his arms out, bracing himself, ready to get a little revenge for the kick in the ribs. Clued in, but still stupid, the guard charged, and Logan used his own weight against him, swinging him by the arm into the wall behind him. Several framed pictures and documents fell to the floor. Logan tsk-tsked.

"Boss ain't gonna like that, big guy."

The guy spun on him, and before it was over, Logan had taken a few of the hard shots he'd anticipated, but he'd won out. The guard lay moaning on the cabin floor, and Logan stood over him, a foot planted securely over his throat. Logan smiled down, applying a little pressure.

"Where are the women that you scum are holding?"

No answer. He pressed down a little, watching the guard's eyes pop a little.

"Where?"

The guard shook his head, no help at all. Logan swore, pulling him up by the coat and hitting him once more, hard, and knocked him cold. He dragged the guard's dead weight over to the corner and tied him securely to a table. All of the furniture was bolted to stay put, so his friend might wake up, but he wasn't going anywhere anytime soon.

Logan fished the computer card out, and pulled out the small transmitter, hoping it worked and they could hear him. He made sure the computer was on, and then inserted the card. Grabbing the phone, he dialed the same number he'd used earlier, feeling triumphant. Ian picked up the phone on the first ring.

"It's done. You can download. Tell me where Sarah is—I couldn't find out if there was anyone else here. Then you can send in the troops."

He heard Ian's voice, scratchy but clear in his small earpiece. "We lost Sarah's signal, Logan. They must have found the transmitter. Find her."

His hands turned to ice as Ian's precise demand hit him over the phone like a hard slap.

"Logan?"

He didn't respond, his mind racing to think of where she could be, what could have happened to her while he'd been waiting around all day. He should have tried to find her first.

"Logan!"

"What?"

"We have her last known position in the room at the end of the hall, stern side. Check there first." Then Ian's voice softened a bit, and Logan could tell Sarah's boss was feeling exactly the same fear in the pit of his stomach that he was. "Let us know the moment you have her."

"I will."

He'd barely hung up before he was out the door.

SARAH SAT CALMLY on the bed, waiting for her "date." They'd moved her to a more luxuriously appointed room, though the bed was obviously the centerpiece. Some sex toys and lotions were set conveniently on the bed stand, and she'd counted at least three cameras. She felt dirty just sitting there, but planned on being the last woman they tried to victimize.

She'd showered and put on the next-to-nothing piece of silk that Valente had left for her—no underwear except for a matching thong. At least the clothes allowed her flexible movement. Certainly, that was for her date's convenience, but she planned on using it to her advantage.

She'd ignored the heels and remained barefoot. She preferred both feet on the floor when she was kicking someone's ass. One of the lethal heels they'd provided was hidden under the pillow—a weapon, just in case. If Logan didn't find a way in, if things went wrong, she'd do what was necessary to protect herself.

But if everything was going according to plan, all hell should break loose soon enough and she'd be out of there.

The day had seemed to last years. She didn't know what time it was, but the sky outside the portal was black. The boat should have been heading slowly back to shore. But for now it was still, but for the gentle rocking of the waves.

The door handle slid down and she held her breath. *Showtime.*

Valente walked through the door with a shorter, fatter, darker man. Sarah wasn't sure what his ethnicity was, but he had cruel eyes. He looked at her and then his eyes flitted to the table, a greasy smile emerging when he saw the things laid out there. He looked at her again, and she wanted to hide. He nodded at Valente, who smiled and shook his hand warmly before looking at Sarah.

"Our guest finds you acceptable." He pinned Sarah with his gaze. "I know you won't disappoint him. He doesn't speak English, but I'm sure he can make known what he wants from you. Do this well, and maybe you'll have satisfied your debt by morning. If not…" He shrugged, and turned to the man, saying something in his language, complete gibberish to Sarah.

Valente closed the door with one more meaningful look in her direction. She barely noticed as she was formulating a plan to deal with this disgusting situation. She didn't want to touch this toad of a man, but she had to take charge to keep the upper hand. No one knew where she was, and until the boat was raided, she was on her own.

She smiled, in what she hoped was a sexy, come-hither way, and lay back on the bed. The toad was practically drooling. It made it hard to not be overcome with disgust; however, as she thought about what she was really going to do, she got a little more in the mood. With all of the cameras on them she had to make this look good, or Valente would have his goons inside within seconds. One fat man she could take; several of Valente's guards, well, that would be more of a challenge.

Her visitor mumbled something as he strolled slowly to the bed, his eyes glued to her as she leaned back, letting one leg hang over the side of the bed while the other perched in a sexy bend on the blankets. Sarah grinned, using her sexiest voice.

"Bring it on over here, big guy. I am so gonna rock your world."

He spewed a muffled little laugh and reached out to touch her thigh appreciatively. She had to bite the inside of her cheek not to kick him in the head out of reflex.

She let him touch, to a point, and then wound her leg around the back of his hip, a move he must have liked very much. She tried to keep as much distance as she could, considering there was only a little bit of silk between them. If she was going to get him where she wanted him, she couldn't be prissy about it.

Then he did exactly what she needed him to do. As he reached down to grab a boob, she caught his forearm midgrope and pulled hard, levering up with all of her strength to roll him quickly over and then rolling over on top of him herself. The little fat man was surprised, but then smiled widely, and those pudgy little hands started to travel.

She tolerated what she had to, leaning down over him, pretending to whisper something in his ear, and forced herself to kiss him—mouth closed—and she hoped to God the cameras couldn't see that she was actually cutting off his blood supply with a sharp pressure from her fist on his carotid artery. He was limp in a second, completely unconscious.

Relief made her sag, too, and she laughed, assuming someone was listening in.

"Well, apparently that was too much for you, hot stuff. Not much for endurance, are you? I'll let you rest a moment, and just see what toys we have on the table over here."

She lifted off the bed carefully, extinguishing the light,

hoping that either no one was watching or they didn't find anything about what had happened suspicious.

She stepped back reflexively as the door handle clunked down and one of Valente's guards stepped in.

No such luck.

14

LOGAN RUSHED down the hall, checking what rooms he could get into, knocking on the doors of others, hoping to hell he would find Sarah behind one of them. She hadn't been in the room where E.J. and Ian had last heard from her. He tried to remain calm, but the truth was she could be anywhere. She could be hurt. Or worse.

He heard a commotion at the end of the hall and slid to the side, sinking into a tiny alcove as he saw two big guys run down the passageway. With guns.

That couldn't be good.

He heard more commotion above him—sounded like the troops had been sent in. Dammit, Ian hadn't held off; Logan's urgency to find Sarah tripled. He had to get to her, and anyone else being held hostage—they'd be in even more danger now that the ship had been boarded.

Dashing back out, he barely took the time to make sure the coast was clear before he ran down the hall shouting her name—why bother trying to be discreet when all hell was about to break loose?

Turning a corner, he slammed into someone, both of them grunting loudly at the contact as he stumbled back, then poised himself to fight whoever was standing in his path.

He blinked once, disbelieving.

Sarah stood opposite him, also in fighting stance, her cheek cut, her hair wild, wearing nothing but some scrap of see-through material that showed almost everything there was to see. Not that she seemed to notice.

He blinked again, thinking he must be hallucinating. Then she grinned.

"I almost took you out, Sullivan. Should watch where you're going."

His voice seemed a little thin and surreal to him as he relaxed his stance, still staring. "I was coming to…uh…"

She grinned even wider. "Save me?"

He could swear he felt heat invading his face, which hadn't happened in so long he couldn't remember. He stepped forward, reached out and touched where her face was bleeding.

"You're hurt."

"A scratch." She shrugged. "The second guy was a little more difficult than the first."

"The second guy?"

His eyes traveled down the passageway past her shoulder, and he saw a man's body lying halfway in and out of the doorway. The guy was big—and knocked out cold. Logan walked past her, feeling a little dazed. As he approached the room, he saw another man, heavyset and balding, lifting up groggily on the bed as if he had no idea where he was.

"You did this?" The incredulity in his own voice

shamed him when he saw the flash of hurt and anger in her blue eyes.

"I told you I am more than capable of taking care of myself. I don't need anyone rescuing me, thanks."

She whipped around and started down the hallway in the opposite direction, and he called out.

"Sarah, the ship's been boarded by the Coast Guard. The place will be swarming in a second."

She didn't break her pace, not getting his hint, so he spelled it out for her.

"You're pretty much naked, sweetheart. In case you didn't realize, you're about to give the U.S. Coast Guard quite a show."

That stopped her. She looked down, and he saw her shoulders stiffen. He had to smile. She was so into the fight, the takedown, she hadn't even thought of what she was wearing. She probably could have taken these guys out buck naked, and his admiration for her rose sharply. What a woman.

He couldn't think of much else as she turned around and came back toward him. He knew with stunning certainty he didn't want another man—let alone a boatload of them—getting the same view he was getting. Ever.

She walked up to him, crouched, and pulled the unconscious guard's jacket roughly from his inert body, slipping into it. It was huge, but covered what was important. As she turned to leave again, he caught her elbow.

"Hey."

"What? I need to get up there. Tell them about these guys. Don't let them go anywhere."

"Believe me, we'll be found soon enough." He ran a hand through his hair, confused, raw and so relieved she was okay that it was almost painful. He didn't want to let her out of his sight.

"I'm sorry I came on like a condescending ass. It's more than evident you don't need anyone to save you."

She apparently had no response to that, and just looked down the hall like she was wishing for the cavalry to show up, but they were still alone. Finally, she looked up.

"Thanks."

Sarah wrapped her arms tightly around her middle. Logan searched for words and ended up sending a silent but threatening look to the man on the bed, sending him scuttling back into the room.

He was just going to reach for her, close the awkward distance between them, when Sarah's face tensed in surprise, and she spit out a curse. Before he could ask her what was the matter, she flew past him, down the hall. Unquestioningly, he followed.

"Sarah, what…?" Then he saw.

Valente.

He was trying to make a break for it with two of his goons, each of them dragging a woman behind him. Rage filled Logan and he picked up the pace, intent on getting his hands on the man who had threatened Sarah and who might finally know what had happened to Mel. Mel was not one of the women whom the men were dragging after them, but maybe…

He caught up with Sarah, easily sprinting beside her

as they dashed after Valente. Their rhythms matched, their breath coming evenly, their attention targeted—it was close to sex, he thought, excitement and the thrill of the chase pulsing through his veins.

They turned the corner and saw Valente disappearing up a small staircase that must lead to a hidden exit. Logan bolted, covering the distance in a flat second. He busted through the pair of guards, sending them flying into the bulkheads, and lunged for Valente's legs, throwing him violently down to the floor.

Valente came up swinging, as did his guards, roughly shoving the women they had been dragging along to the floor and taking on the three-against-two battle. In minutes it was over, the guards out cold on the floor. Valente tried to rise, his eyes widening as he saw Logan and Sarah looming over him. Sarah checked on the women, and looked at Logan with concerned eyes.

"They're heavily drugged. They'll need medical care fast."

Logan grabbed Valente by the neck and lifted him, slamming him up against the wall. He looked back at Sarah with a question in his eyes. She met his eyes as she tried to prop the women's sagging forms somehow comfortably against the bulkhead, and just said, in her heaviest Brooklyn accent, "I don't see nuthin'."

Valente swung, striking out hard, and Logan ducked the punch, shoving his adversary back hard against the wall, getting in his face.

"I'm going to show you a picture. It's of someone I

know. If you tell me what you know about her, maybe I'll let you go without any bones being broken."

Valente's too-handsome features paled as Logan reached into his jacket pocket, pulling out a picture of Mel. Valente nodded, a smirk sliding over his sweaty face.

"Yeah, I can tell you about her. She was real good." He lifted his chin, meeting Logan's look with a sleazy glare. "*Real* good. Much better than these two put together." He peered at the dazed women on the floor. "Had to have a sample of your friend for myself, if you know what I mean."

Logan slammed a fist into the man's gut, wiping the leering look off his face, and brought him back up against the wall, gasping.

"Where is she? What did you do with her?"

No matter what horrible things had obviously happened, Logan felt a small glimmer of hope that Mel could still be alive. Somewhere. Valente crushed that hope with his response.

"She's gone. Had to get rid of her. She'd cooperate as long as we kept her loose—"

"You drugged her, too?"

Valente just smiled again, a vile light in his eyes. "Yeah, and she was a real party girl when she was stoned."

Logan hauled off to slam him again, but his arm was caught midswing. Sarah's strong grip held him back. She held his gaze with her own, urging him to hold back. To get control. He nodded, expelling a haggard breath, and she turned to Valente.

"You killed her, then?"

"Yeah. So what? One more worthless—"

Sarah let go of Logan's arm and Logan hit him again—hard—before he stood back. Sarah put her hand on his arm, taking over.

"Well, pal, you are going to prison for a very, very long time. You kidnapped, raped and tortured several women, but this one—" she took the picture from Logan. "—happened to be a cop. Just. Like. Me." She accentuated every last word with a jab of her finger into his chest, but held off hitting him herself. She didn't want to get her hands dirty.

Valente paled as they heard voices emerging down at the far end of the passageway.

"Your word against mine."

"Oh yeah, there's a problem. But not quite. You just confessed. And we have two witnesses right here, did you forget?"

"So it's the word of a bunch of drugged up party girls against mine."

"Not exactly." Logan chimed in, reaching into his pocket again, pulling out the transmitter. "You gave the nice policemen listening in back home a recorded confession."

Valente's face contorted with rage as Coast Guard officers ran down the hall, and Logan and Sarah backed off, hands up, identifying themselves. The lead man nodded while others hauled Valente away.

"We'd been alerted you were here—got a bit worried when we didn't see you at first, but apparently you were busy netting the big fish."

Valente was still yelling and struggling as they carried him off down the passageway. Logan sighed with relief.

"Catch of the day."

15

"HARRY, I THINK YOU'RE SET." Sarah stood up from the terminal where she'd been sitting for several hours, making sure the inn's computer was as secure as it could possibly be. She'd never told him it was Logan who'd been hacking into their connection from upstairs—no need for them to know that. But now no one would be able to mess with their online system, or they would have a heck of a hard time trying.

"We can't thank you enough. Are you sure we can't pay you? I can't imagine what having a private consultant come in here and do all this for us would cost."

Sarah shook her head. She had developed a weakness for Harry; something in his happy eyes reminded her of her grandfather. And Karen made the best pie ever.

"No problem. This is fun for me, really. I'm glad to help."

"We did refund the charges for your vacation stay, at least. You weren't here the full time, even." He sat down at the computer station, checking over his new updates. "You never did say where you disappeared to."

She nodded. "Family emergency."

"That's too bad. I hope everything was all right."

"Don't worry. We had a happy ending, more or less."

"Good to hear. And you are staying for the party later, I take it?"

Sarah nodded. Ian and Sage were finally getting married—the engagement was official, the date set—and they had hired the inn to cater a party to announce their decision to everyone, as well as the news of their impending parenthood. Pretty much everyone already knew, but the party and the announcement would make it official. Sarah had a room for the night, as all guests did, and was looking forward to the celebration. Mostly.

It had been close to a week since they'd taken Valente down, and more than four days since she'd seen or heard from Logan. He'd contacted her before he left—it wasn't like he'd left her high and dry—but the lack of contact, her uncertainty about their future, was bugging her. To say the least.

She couldn't escape the fact that after what had happened on the boat, she'd been hopeful, for the first time in her life, that Logan could lay his past to rest and accept her work. That he would realize she was good at what she did, and that he would see they had something worth sticking around for.

They had both come to the relationship with pain and baggage, and she was ready to deal with hers if he could handle his. They could lend each other a hand and make the burdens lighter together.

She smiled, accepting a slice of pie from Karen before her host fluttered off to attend to some other guests, and she watched Harry mess with the computer, intent on the screen, her presence forgotten. Computer addicts came in all ages, she thought, smiling, before her thoughts returned to Logan.

He'd gone back to face the consequences of his actions on his job. He'd wanted to make sure his partner received honors and a proper service, and he wanted to contact her family. Sarah felt a surge of tenderness nearly overwhelm her, thinking of how important those things were to him, how decent he was. He'd stayed to make sure that the women they'd rescued were put in good treatment programs, and that there weren't any more of them around.

Going through that process with Logan inspired emotions she'd never realized she could feel, but she didn't know what to do now. She was restless, anxious and impatient to have him back so she could see him. Talk to him. Touch him.

Her fingers itched to run themselves over his skin again. But if it was more than lust—love, maybe?—she didn't know. She needed him to help her figure it out.

The pie was gone, and Harry was sucked into his spreadsheets. Late afternoon sunlight dappled through the window, and she tried to shake the lonely feeling that suddenly hit her. Maybe she was tired—she had time for a nap before the party.

"I'll see you tonight, Harry."

"Mmm-hmm."

A few people were standing around talking, but Sarah just wanted to retire to her room to think and recharge her batteries. As she reached the stairs, she was surprised to see Ivy through the screen door, lost in a hot clinch with…Jim. *Jim?* Sarah turned her head. She had tried her best to warn Ivy, but everyone was entitled to their own mistakes. But before her foot hit the first step, she heard the door close, and Ivy's cheerful voice called after her.

"Sarah—wait. I've been looking for you for days! Where have you been?"

"Oh, I had to get back home for a few days."

"Oh, um," Ivy blushed prettily, and Sarah waited for her to continue. "I guess you saw me kissing Jim. You must wonder what that was about."

"No, it's none of my business, Ivy. In fact, I was kind of hoping I might see you, I wanted to apologize for being so hard on you the other day—"

Ivy was shaking her head vehemently. "No, really, you were right. But more than that, you made me get a grip and stop moping around." She laughed, putting her hand on Sarah's arm in a friendly gesture that seemed very adult. "You made me see that I didn't have to take that kind of treatment from any guy."

Okay, now Sarah was really confused. "But, you were just…"

"Right! I was so angry I went and confronted him, and really let him know how I felt, that no one was going to use me. And then we got talking—it turned out that girl was an old girlfriend, she came back to make a play for him, and that was what I saw. But he swore he was only interested in me. Really."

Sarah felt the old cynicism rear its head, and squelched it. It wasn't her place to rain on Ivy's parade. "Well, I hope that's true and it works out for you, Ivy. I really do."

"Thanks. He's taking me to meet his family this weekend—I'm so nervous. He's never taken anyone to meet them before. And he said he knows he flirts a lot in his job, but he won't do it anymore because I don't like it."

Ivy was literally glowing with happiness. It was hard to resist her excitement, and Sarah didn't try, smiling back and reaching over to hug her.

"That is great news. But just remember to take care of you first, okay?"

"Absolutely—I'm so glad I met you, Sarah. I never would have been brave enough to talk to Jim or stand up for myself if it hadn't been for you." She blushed again, leaning in close. "And Jim says he thinks strong women are sexy, can you believe it? He thinks I'm a strong woman."

"You are."

Sarah smiled again, wishing Ivy luck and excusing herself. Finally she made it upstairs, feeling more worn-out than she had been before, for some reason. She was happy for Ivy, but even though many of her own scars had healed and the pain from her past had faded, new pains had taken their place. Feeling even more tired, she thought of Mel, of the hard road to recovery the two women they had rescued faced, and of Logan's obvious doubts about their relationship. She wasn't convinced of happy endings just yet.

Stepping into the room, she was struck immediately by a strong, sweet scent that made her mouth water. At the foot of the bed was a large, white wicker basket over-flowing with large, ripe peaches. They hadn't been there earlier....

Her heart hammered in her chest as the memory of telling Logan about her peaches and sex fantasy rose to her mind. Just then, he stepped out from the bathroom as if she'd wished him into existence. He was wearing only his jeans, the rest of him bare and freshly show-ered. He met her surprised gaze, grinned in a slanted, sexy way and threw his damp towel on the chair.

"Hi. I hope you don't mind me using your shower. I just got in a few minutes ago. You looked busy, so Karen let me in." His eyes communicated a bit of doubt, and he looked down, then back at her again. "I told her not to say anything—I wanted to surprise you. I hope that's okay."

She didn't say anything—she didn't know what to say—and just stood in place like an idiot, staring at his gorgeous torso, trying not to race across the room and jump him. What was it about a guy dressed only in jeans that could erase any coherent thoughts from a woman's mind?

He solved the problem by pulling her into a deep em-brace, swallowing her thoughts with a kiss so hot she was sure that her bones melted. His breath warmed her skin as he spoke against her mouth, barely lifting his lips from hers.

"I missed you."

She smiled a little, unable to repress the happy flutterings his words brought forth.

"I missed you, too."

She knew they had to talk, there had been so much left unsaid between them when he'd had to leave, but she was far too aware of the hot skin of his chest pressed up against her hungry, aroused body.

Leaning forward, she pressed a tender kiss to his jaw, and then his shoulder. She darted her tongue out to taste him and moved her fingers lightly over his back. He groaned and found her mouth again, his hands everywhere. Spinning her around, he kicked the door shut with his foot and eyed the basket of peaches with intent.

Her breath came a little faster at the thought of licking the sweet, sticky juice of the ripe fruit from his skin, and thinking about him doing the same for her, but she took a deep breath, getting her hormones under control.

"What happened in Baltimore?"

He sighed, resting his forehead against hers. "There's nothing keeping me there now."

"They fired you? Even though you solved the case?" She was indignant for him and he chuckled softly, running his fingers over her hair tenderly.

"*We* solved the case, and the bust went to your department. That's fine with me—I couldn't have done it without you."

She wondered what saying that had cost him, and raised her hand to his face as he continued. "They let me quit, giving me my retirement funds and even paying me for lost sick and vacation time. It was the right thing for everyone. I did what I needed to do. Made sure Mel's reputation was cleared, and that she was memorialized with honors."

"It must be so hard for her family, for you and everyone, just having her disappear like that. You know, we made sure none of those pictures of her will appear ever again, anywhere. And if they do, we'll know."

He nodded. "Thanks for that. It will be difficult for her family for a while. I plan to stay in touch, to help them out if I can."

Sarah's heart swelled, and she pushed back tears. Enough was enough—she wasn't going to go all girly just because she had feelings for Logan.

"So what are you going to do now?"

He ran the back of his fingers down her bare arm, eliciting shivers of the best kind.

"Right now, I am exactly where I want to be." He kissed her softly. "I know we have some things to talk about, but I want to look for work down here. To be with you, near you."

"So my job doesn't bother you anymore?"

He traced his finger along the light line on her cheek that still showed a very faint bruise and cut from where she'd been clipped in battle just the week before. His eyes darkened, and he sighed. "It bothers me. It will always bother me to see you hurt, to know you're in danger."

He felt her stiffen a little in his arms, and smiled, massaging her shoulders, adding, "But I'm pretty sure that I'm crazy in love with you, too, and I'm willing to work on dealing with my anxiety about your work. You're not only good at your job and capable of handling things yourself—you're amazing at it. That makes me worry a lot less."

The smile that stole over her face filled her eyes and, by extension, his heart. She whispered, "I think I'm crazy in love with you, too. Fighting with you—and being away from you—has really sucked."

He laughed—he couldn't have said it better himself. His heart hadn't felt this full, this alive, for as long as he could remember. Loving Sarah breathed new life into him, and that was enough to combat the fear he felt about the risks she took in her job. He didn't want to change anything about her, he realized, even that.

"And what about you? What are you going to do?"

He stepped back, walking to the window across from the end of the bed.

"I thought I might open my own business. I've saved a lot of money over the years. I'm not sure doing what yet—building boats, maybe, or some kind of construction. I went into law enforcement mostly to have some kind of connection with my dad, I think. And besides, if things go the way I hope, and we have a family someday—"

"Whoa, hold on there—"

He just laughed again. "I said someday, sweetheart, not right now. Relax. I'm just saying, having one of us in a dangerous profession is enough. I don't need to be a cop anymore. One in the family will be plenty."

She crossed to where he stood, shaking her head in

wonder. "I guess I just never really thought about having all that—family, I mean. It just blows my mind—hell, I never even thought about having this, someone like you, in my life. Let's just take it one step at a time."

"Sounds good."

"So what's the next step?"

He kissed her, walking her back toward the bed. "How much time do we have before the party starts?" he asked, reaching for a peach.

THERE WAS no threat of rain as the party went into full swing, and E.J. was in high spirits. He was thrilled for his friends, watching Ian standing protectively by Sage's side. She hid her irritation at his hovering well, E.J. thought with a smile. Love could make you tolerant of a lot of things that normally would drive you crazy. At least that's what his mother had always claimed about his father—usually when he was driving her crazy. The memory was bittersweet. His dad had been gone several years now, but he still thought of him every day.

His eyes caught Logan and Sarah as they emerged from the building, two hours late and looking well and freshly loved—it wasn't exactly a secret what had detained them. Sarah's expression was luminous, shining with just the kind of happiness he'd wished for her.

He felt soft fingers at his nape and smiled, turning to his date. Grabbing Lori's hand, he lifted it to his mouth, looking into her pretty blue eyes, and drew his tongue over her palm—delicious. He'd met her the day before, when he was registering a new car at the DMV. He'd always wanted a convertible, and so finally he'd gone out and bought the sweetest little BMW 6-series you could imagine. Later on, he'd gone back by the office when Lori got off shift and had taken her to dinner to celebrate his new purchase, right on the shiny, curvy hood.

Life was good. He was happy for his friends, and enjoyed social occasions, but the look in this woman's eyes told him she wanted to be alone. Who was he to argue?

Sarah's sardonic, teasing whisper in his ear broke the spell. "They do have rooms here, Beaumont."

He could swear she smelled like fresh Georgia peaches, and raised an eyebrow as he turned to see her and Logan hand in hand.

"I know—I booked the one over yours." He grinned wickedly. "It's good to see you. I wondered if you were going to make it down here." He raised his eyebrows teasingly at Sarah and almost laughed when her cheeks turned bright pink.

Man, she had it bad.

"Good to see you again, too, E.J.—under better circumstances. Last time you were busy charging Valente and some of his men, so we really didn't get to meet properly." Logan held out his hand, and E.J. gripped it firmly. "I wanted to thank you. For all of your help."

E.J. shook his head. "It was all Sarah. We were just the backup team this time."

She blushed a little more, but when she caught his stare, her eyes narrowed. She was ready to square off—it was good to know that Sarah smitten with love was still Sarah—so he took a different approach, reaching for her hand and lifting it to his mouth for a light kiss.

"Sarah, you look breathtaking. And I am so proud of the work you did out there. I imagine Logan is, too." He cast a knowing look in Logan's direction, hoping the man did indeed appreciate the jewel he had found in Sarah.

Her jaw practically dropped and it was all he could do to keep a straight face at her reaction, but it was also true. Sarah was beautiful under normal circumstances, but dressed in a simple white sundress, softened by love and the golden lights that illuminated the yard, she was stunning.

He reached over for Lori's hand, not wanting her to feel ignored. Lori knew they were just having fun, but that didn't mean he wasn't going to treat her like any gentleman should treat the lady he was out with.

She scooted up beside him, squeezing his fingers, and offered her friendly congratulations to everyone. E.J. smiled down at her, glad she didn't mind hanging out with his friends. Another voice broke into the mix.

"Don't worry, Logan, Sarah is resistant to that suave southern charm."

E.J. cocked an eyebrow as Ian walked up behind, landing a firm grip on Logan's shoulder, reintroducing himself as well, and receiving Logan's hearty congratulations on his impending fatherhood. Ian was in rare form himself, it seemed.

"So, Logan, are you looking for a job? I think we could put in a word for you."

Logan just shook his head and looked at Sarah, smiling slightly before turning his attention back to Ian. E.J. barely heard as Logan politely declined Ian's offer, and the conversation turned to babies and various shoptalk. Normally he would have laughed at how the two men wanted to talk about babies and Sarah kept bringing the conversation back to work, but right now he just wanted to escape. He wanted to leave before everyone started telling him, as couples were wont to do, that he should start thinking about making a permanent match with someone. And Lori was stroking his wrist in a most intriguing manner....

And while he was happy for his friends, he was enjoying his life just the way it was. No marriage or babies for him. He'd dodged that bullet once, and didn't intend to get serious about anyone anytime soon. *No sir-ee.*

The party picked up, champagne flowing freely, music carrying through the humid summer night. Ian and Sage made their happy announcements to everyone's applause, and E.J. thought the moment was just right to sweep his date up to their room for a party of their own.

As he whispered in Lori's ear, feeling her lean into him in a way that said she had no objections whatsoever to his plans, he hooked his arm around her shoulders and kissed her in such a way that she was already moaning softly into his mouth, but he didn't feel quite as thrilled as he'd anticipated.

What did he expect?

He saw many women, and some excited him more

than others. Everyone was different, and he couldn't expect more than was being offered. It was easier to push any doubts away and forge ahead. And that's what he told himself as they rose and headed to his room. He was calling it a night for now.

* * * * *

Look for EJ's compelling story in November 2007, when Book 3 of the HOTWIRES mini-series is released: Flirtation by Samantha Hunter. And don't forget to check out her website at www.samanthahunter.com.

2 FREE

BOOKS AND A SURPRISE GIFT!

We would like to take this opportunity to thank you for reading this Mills & Boon® book by offering you the chance to take TWO more specially selected titles from the Blaze® series absolutely FREE! We're also making this offer to introduce you to the benefits of the Mills & Boon® Reader Service™—

- ★ **FREE home delivery**
- ★ **FREE gifts and competitions**
- ★ **FREE monthly Newsletter**
- ★ **Exclusive Reader Service offers**
- ★ **Books available before they're in the shops**

Accepting these FREE books and gift places you under no obligation to buy, you may cancel at any time, even after receiving your free shipment. Simply complete your details below and return the entire page to the address below. You don't even need a stamp!

YES! Please send me 2 free Blaze books and a surprise gift. I understand that unless you hear from me, I will receive 4 superb new titles every month for just £3.10 each, postage and packing free. I am under no obligation to purchase any books and may cancel my subscription at any time. The free books and gift will be mine to keep in any case.

K7ZED

Ms/Mrs/Miss/Mr ....Initials ....
BLOCK CAPITALS PLEASE

Surname ....

Address ....

....

....Postcode...

Send this whole page to:
UK: FREEPOST CN81, Croydon, CR9 3WZ